S0-CPB-903

TOMORROW CITY

Praise for *Tomorrow City*:

A tight, tense crime novel about a stranger in a strange land trying to outrun the ghosts of his past. Kirk Kjeldsen's Shanghai is a terrifically fresh and evocative setting, and the action jumps off the page.

> - Lou Berney, Edgar Award and Barry Award-
> nominated author of *Whiplash River*
> and *Gutshot Straight*

Tomorrow City is a vicious little tale of men and violence and the sucking black hole of the past. A coiled and sleek throwback noir, best read in one shot. More please.

> - Elwood Reid, author of *If I Don't Six*,
> *Midnight Sun*, and *D.B.*

Tomorrow City unfolds with grace and power, building to a cinematic climax that reverberates long after you've finished reading. This is thriller writing at its finest. Kjeldsen is one to watch.

> - Carlo Bernard, screenwriter of *The Great Raid*,
> *Prince of Persia: The Sands of Time*,
> and *The Uninvited*

In *Tomorrow City*, the dark past of a former American criminal catches up with him in the chaotic streets of Shanghai. Exciting action in an exotic setting. Read. You'll enjoy.

> - Tom Epperson, Edgar Award and
> Barry Award-nominated author of
> *The Kind One* and *Sailor*

A fascinating and exciting read by a talented newcomer.

- Victor Gischler, Edgar Award-nominated
author of *Gun Monkeys* and *The Deputy*

Tomorrow City is darn near a perfect book—fierce, intelligent, gritty, and absolutely convincing. You can certainly count me as a fan of Kirk Kjeldsen.

- Martin Clark, author of *The Legal Limit*

I had a twofold pleasure in reading Kjeldsen's debut. As a writer, I admired his skill at evoking a sense of place and his uncommon ability to evoke sympathy for a criminal. But the real payoff came as a reader: *Tomorrow City* is *such* a cracking good story.

- Leighton Gage, author of *Perfect Hatred*,
Blood of the Wicked, and
Every Bitter Thing

Kirk Kjeldsen jabs a needle into the soft spot where nightmares intersect with real life and injects a steady dose of speed. *Tomorrow City* is a relentless, surprising and harrowing tour of the fascinating underside of Shanghai.

- David Rich, author of *Caravan of Thieves*

Kirk Kjeldsen has written a one-sitting novel with an ex-con protagonist you'll eagerly follow across the globe as he tries to shake his past. *Tomorrow City* is as exciting as it is smart as it is heartbreaking.

- Michael Kardos, author of *The Three Day Affair*

TOMORROW CITY

A novel

KIRK KJELDSEN

Signal 8 Press
Hong Kong

Tomorrow City
By Kirk Kjeldsen
Published by Signal 8 Press
An imprint of Typhoon Media Ltd
Copyright 2013 Kirk Kjeldsen
ISBN: 978-988-15542-1-5
eISBN: 978-988-15542-5-3

Typhoon Media Ltd
Signal 8 Press | BookCyclone | Lightning Originals
Hong Kong
www.typhoon-media.com

All rights reserved. No part of this book may be reproduced in any form or by any means, except for brief citation or review, without written permission from Typhoon Media Ltd.

This is a work of fiction. Names, characters, places, and incidents are either products of the author's imagination or are used fictitiously. Any resemblance to actual events, locales, organizations, or persons, living or dead, is entirely coincidental and beyond the intent of either the author or the publisher.

Cover image: Justin Kowalczuk
Author photo: Philip Gostelow

RO441352711

*for Lauren
and Amalie*

"tomorrow is our permanent address and there they'll scarcely find us"

-E.E. Cummings

CONTENTS

CHAPTER ONE

NEW YORK CITY
MAY 1998

BRENDAN Lavin woke with a start to the metallic crash of an empty trash dumpster being slammed to the ground. He looked over at the radio alarm clock, which was blaring some grating Matchbox Twenty song. The time was 6:17 AM, which meant that the alarm had been going off for almost three hours. The bed next to him was empty. Maureen was still at the hospital, working another overnight shift.

"Fuck!"

He jumped out of bed and pulled on a dirty t-shirt and a rumpled pair of chef's pants. Then he rushed out of his apartment, stopping once along the way to shove his bare feet into his sneakers. He sprinted the five blocks to his small bakery, which occupied a tiny, rundown storefront on Ditmars Avenue. In the distance to the east, the maraschino-colored sun was appearing on the horizon. A young woman was jogging on the opposite side of the street in the direction of the Hell Gate Bridge, and across the way, a man was dropping off newspapers at the C-Town.

When he got to the bakery, Brendan realized that he had forgotten his key. It wasn't the first time. In fact, it had happened frequently enough for him to wonder if this was just his unconscious trying to keep his old skill set up to snuff. From loose dirt and gravel along the base of the building, he fished out a snaky, gleaming wire. He knelt, angled this tool into the lock, and waited for that old popping sound, as familiar to him as the voice of a childhood friend.

That foolishness behind him, he hurried inside and turned on the used convection oven he'd purchased the year before at a forfeiture auction in Long Island. He stole a glance at the scuffed face of the wall clock—it was already almost six-thirty, which meant that the oven wouldn't be pre-heated until at least a quarter to seven, almost three hours behind schedule. The fourteen-hour days were getting to him, and he no longer had the Adderall and Ritalin to help. He had gotten clean while incarcerated at Rikers.

He hurried around the kitchen in a half-asleep, half-awake daze, pulling out buckets of prepared dough from the refrigerator, taking down mixing bowls and dry ingredients off the shelves. The crude tattoo of a tiger crouched on the inside of his left forearm as he worked. He pulled the towels and plastic wrap off the bucket tops and pounded the dough before setting it aside to start on batters for the scones and muffins. He ended up spilling so much milk, sugar, and flour that he could've made something else from all of the ingredients that ended up on the floor.

Before long, Brendan heard a knock at the back door. He looked over toward the oven—still a hundred degrees away from being pre-heated. After a moment, there was another knock at the back door, followed by the gruff voice of a heavy smoker.

"Hey, Brendan? You in there?"

Brendan ignored the voice and continued with his preparations. After a moment, the person pounded against the door.

"I see the lights on," said the person. "Come on, open up."

Brendan stopped what he was doing and went over to open the door. Pat O'Brien, a plug of a man in his fifties, stood out in the alley by an idling Chevy van, chewing on an unlit cheroot cigar.

"Where's the fuck's my bread?" he said, spitting the words through yellowed teeth.

"I'm running a little behind," said Brendan.

"That's the third time this month."

"I'll make it up to you, I promise."

"Fuck this."

Pat turned and walked back toward his van. Brendan hurried out the door after him.

"Wait," he said. "I'll give you a discount. I'll even throw in some free rolls—"

Before Brendan could finish, Pat got into his van and drove off. Brendan stood there for a moment and watched the van disappear down the alley.

Then he smelled something burning in the kitchen.

He spent his entire morning splitting his time between the kitchen and the register out front. Business was slow.

For the first ten months he'd been open, he had been able to pay a middle-aged Ecuadorian woman to work the counter for him, but sales had been so dismal that he had recently had to let her go. Behind on his payments to his suppliers, he was in danger of not making his next rent payment as well.

Business during the afternoon turned out to be even worse than it had been in the morning. Brendan listened to *Mike and the Mad Dog* while he went through his pile of overdue bills. He barely had enough money left in his checking account to pay for just one of them. The phone was the first thing that would be cut off, but he figured he could get by on his cell phone for a while if he had to. Instead, he'd pay the electricity bill. Without electricity, there would be no bread.

Just before three in the afternoon, a heavyset man in a business suit entered the bakery. He wore leather driving gloves and seemed nimble on his feet for a man his size.

"You guys do muffins?"

"Yeah," said Brendan, pointing to the display case. "We've got corn, blueberry, and raisin bran."

"No chocolate chip or anything?"

"No."

"Are any of them low-fat?"

"No, but we only use fresh ingredients here."

"Give me a blueberry one. And a large coffee."

Brendan placed a blueberry muffin in a brown paper bag and filled a large paper cup with coffee.

"Three bucks," he said.

The man paid him with a five-dollar bill. Brendan gave the man his change.

"You want to compete with Dunkin' Donuts, you should think about having more flavors," said the man. "Chocolate chip. Cinnamon swirl. That sort of thing."

Brendan forced a smile.

"I'll keep that in mind," he said, as the man left the store. Then he looked down into the open cash register.

There wasn't even enough money to take Maureen out to Red Lobster.

At four o'clock, Brendan got a broom from the closet in back and began to sweep up the bakery. Before he got halfway through, a black Chevy Camaro IROC-Z with tinted windows pulled to the curb outside. Tommy Donnelly got out of the car and approached the bakery's front door. He wore jeans and a flannel shirt and had the flattened nose of a boxer.

Brendan felt like throwing up when he saw Tommy. He liked Maureen's second cousin even more than she did, but he was afraid of him as well. Tommy was part of the crew that Brendan had robbed warehouses and sixteen-wheelers with, and he had been avoiding them ever since his arrest for a failed job in Staten Island. They had taken care of him while he was in prison and had sent him cigarettes and protection money; in turn, he had kept his mouth shut. As far as he was concerned, they were even. He wanted nothing more to do with them.

Tommy entered the store and approached the counter. Brendan regarded him warily, keeping an eye on the sidewalk out front.

"What's up, bro?" said Tommy.

"What are you doing here?" asked Brendan.

"It's good to see you, too," said Tommy. "How's business?"

Brendan said nothing. Tommy looked around the bakery.

"Where are all your customers?" he asked. "It's like a ghost town in here."

"You come all the way over here just to rag on me?"

"Hell, no," said Tommy. "I came to get some crullers."

"Seriously?"

"Yeah. This is a bakery, ain't it?"

Brendan reached for a paper bag.

"How many you want?" he asked.

"How many you got?"

Brendan counted them.

"Seven," he said.

"I'll take them all."

Tommy pointed to the scones.

"Give me a bunch of those, too," he said. "And give me some muffins."

"For real?"

"I'm making a run for the guys," said Tommy. "We've been working all day over at Ducie's—"

Brendan stopped filling the bag and cut him off.

"I'm not interested," he said.

"Not interested in what?"

"Whatever it is you're going to try to sell me."

"But you haven't even heard it yet."

"I don't need to."

"Brendan—"

"I'm done with that shit. You know that."

"This job's really sweet," said Tommy.

"Then you shouldn't have any trouble finding someone else."

"Come on," he said. "Ducie likes you."

"Fuck Ducie."

"Brendan—"

"I told you, I'm not interested."

"All right."

Brendan finished filling the bag of pastries and shoved it to Tommy.

"Sixteen bucks."

Tommy took the bag of pastries and paid for them with a crisp, new hundred-dollar bill.

"You change your mind, give me a call," he said. "A job like this could go a long way toward helping you keep this place afloat."

Before Brendan could get him his change, Tommy turned and left the bakery. Brendan watched him get back into the IROC-Z and drive off. After Tommy was gone, he looked down at the hundred-dollar bill.

His hands hadn't trembled this badly since the morning he had been processed into Rikers.

CHAPTER TWO

BRENDAN walked home the long way, passing through Astoria Park. He stopped halfway through and watched the sun set over the Manhattan skyline. A few teenagers were passing around a joint over by the rundown Olympic swimming pool. For a brief moment, Brendan wished he could be fifteen again, before the first time he'd been sent away to Tryon, but the moment didn't last. A few minutes later, the sun disappeared over the horizon.

He got up and walked home. It was dark by the time he got back to his apartment. Maureen was there; it was her day off. Red-haired and beautiful in a relaxed, natural way, she was asleep on their fold-out futon bed, one of the dog-eared nursing textbooks she'd bought secondhand from the St. Paul's School of Nursing bookstore in her lap. Still as surprised that she was with him now as he'd been back in high school, when they had started dating, Brendan watched her sleep for a moment.

Then he picked her up and carried her into the bedroom.

When the alarm went off at three o'clock, Brendan woke up feeling as if he'd just closed his eyes. He quickly shut it off and dressed quietly so that he would not wake Maureen. As soon as he was finished dressing, he made his way to the door and left the apartment.

He got to the bakery at three-thirty. The oven was preheated by a quarter to four; by four-thirty, the first loaves of *vollkornbrot* and sourdough rye were already coming out, their golden crowns cracked and split open. After he loaded more bread into the oven, he began preparing batters for scones, muffins, doughnuts, and other pastries, using the recipes given to him by Richie Fusaro, one of his favorite instructors from the Fresh Start Program back at Rikers and the closest thing to a father he had ever had. When he ran out of sugar, he used the rest of his flour to mix up dough for dinner rolls and put it aside to rise. At five, he went outside to wait for Nicky Giordano, one of his suppliers, but when Nicky hadn't shown up by five-fifteen, Brendan took out his cell phone. After a few rings, Nicky answered. It sounded like he was in a crowded kitchen.

"What do you want?"

"Where's my stuff?" asked Brendan.

"I told you. You don't pay, I don't deliver."

"I'll get you the money, I promise."

"I can't pay my bills on promises."

"Please—"

"Sorry," he said. "Call me when you got my money."

He hung up before Brendan could reply.

Brendan called back, but it went straight to voice-mail. He hung up and went back into the bakery, where he unlocked the safe underneath the counter. He had about sixty dollars and a few rolls of change, enough to buy the ingredients he needed to last through the morning.

He had another couple hundred dollars in his bank account, but he knew it wouldn't get him through the week.

That day, he sold only about a quarter of the things that he'd baked. After he closed, he gave the items that were about to go bad to the homeless men who stayed at the Salvation Army on Steinway. He'd been doing that since he had gone into business, preferring that his bread go to use rather than be thrown away. Besides, if there was such a thing a karma, he figured, he'd welcome any help he could get.

He headed back to his apartment building. When he got there, he got his mail from the mailbox in the lobby. Under the junk—circulars for C-Town, Costco, and the new Bed Bath & Beyond that was opening in Sunnyside—he found a letter from John Lekas, the man who rented him the space for his bakery. Lekas wanted to increase his rent.

Brendan went inside his apartment. Maureen was already gone, at the hospital again on another overnight shift. He took out his cell phone and punched in John's number. After a few rings, John answered.

"Hello?"

"John? It's Brendan."

"What's up?"

"What's with the increase in rent?"

"Your lease is up."

"So?"

"So this is a popular area. Lots of people are moving out here from Manhattan. They're gonna put in a Starbucks soon."

"Come on."

"Sorry."

"This is bullshit."

"Things change. You don't like it, you're welcome to leave when the lease is up."

"Cut me a break, will you?"

"I'm sorry."

Brendan hung up. After a long moment, he started dialing Tommy's number, which he still knew by heart, even though it had been years since he had used it.

Halfway through dialing, Brendan stopped, closed the phone, and put it away. He glanced around the cramped apartment: everything in it seemed dilapidated. The fabric on the futon from Goodwill was pilling and fraying. The walls were bare, aside from a few photographs in cheap frames from Target. His shoes looked like they belonged to a homeless man, and so did the ill-fitting jacket that he had gotten from a knockoff shop on Steinway.

Brendan took out his cell phone again. He dialed Tommy's number.

After a few rings, Tommy answered.

CHAPTER THREE

THE parking lot outside the Buccaneer Diner in East Elmhurst was filled with Chryslers and Lincoln Town Cars, the vehicles of locals and retirees there to load up on pancakes and eggs before the start of the workday. Nearby, rush-hour traffic choked all four lanes of Astoria Boulevard, and the sidewalks were filled with people on their way to work or school or coming off overnight shifts.

Inside the diner, Ducie Callaghan sat at a large table, packing an unopened box of Marlboros against his palm and occasionally glancing at a wristwatch. He was tall and muscular, built like a power forward. To his right, like a darkened and extended shadow version of Ducie, sat D'Brickashaw Jefferson, also known as Whale. A former Hofstra lineman who weighed over three hundred pounds, Whale was tucking into two separate orders of chicken and waffles, and the diner's silverware looked like children's utensils in his beefy fists. On the other side of Ducie sat Sean Chen, a half-Irish, half-Chinese twenty-four-year-old with a mop of inky black hair and colorful *irezumi* tattoo sleeves covering his arms. Across from Ducie sat Tommy and J.J. Witek, who was built like a linebacker and had frost-tipped hair and a chinstrap beard. They all wore

hooded sweatshirts, Carhartt work jackets, and other anon-
ymous, blue-collar attire. They looked like dock workers or
a construction crew rather than the ex-cons and criminals
they actually were.

J.J. shook his head as he watched Sean shovel a spoonful
of nuclear-colored cereal into his mouth.

"How can you eat that shit?" he asked.

"What?"

"Fucking Froot Loops."

"What's wrong with Froot Loops?"

"What are you, five or something?"

"Piss off."

"Why don't you eat something real?" said J.J., gesturing
to his plate of sausage and biscuits in a viscous gray gravy.

"You mean like those lips and ass patties you're eating?"

"This is a breakfast of fucking champions here."

"More like Chris Farley's last meal."

"Fuck you."

"Where the hell's Brendan?" said Ducie, checking his
watch again.

"Relax," said Tommy. "He'll be here."

"Who do I have blow in here to get some more fucking
coffee?" said Sean, glancing around the diner.

"I'd start with old Zorba over there," said Tommy,
nodding to an overweight manager standing at the counter.
Sean waved but failed to get his attention.

"Anyone watch HBO last night?" asked J.J.

Whale grunted.

"That new DeNiro movie was on," said J.J.

"*Cop Land*?" asked Tommy.

"No, the one about the spin doctor and the producer who make up a war."

"That sucked," said Sean.

"I thought it was all right," said J.J.

"He hasn't done shit since *Raging Bull*."

"What about *Goodfellas*?"

"That's one decent film in almost twenty years. And it wasn't even his movie, either. It was Ray Liotta's. He was just a supporting character."

"What about *Heat*, then?"

Sean shot him an angry glance.

"Please," he said through another mouthful of Froot Loops. "He was phoning that shit in."

"And *Casino*?"

"Come on, that was just *Goodfellas* lite."

"Get the fuck out of here."

After he finished his own breakfast, Whale nodded toward Tommy's plate of barely touched eggs.

"You gonna eat that?" he asked.

Tommy shook his head.

"Help yourself," he said.

He pushed the plate of half-eaten eggs toward Whale. J.J. turned to see Brendan approaching their table, wearing a black watch cap and an oil-stained mechanic's jacket. There were dark rings underneath his eyes, and it looked like he hadn't slept.

"Well, well," said J.J. "Look what the cat dragged in."

"Where the fuck have you been?" asked Ducie.

"Nice to see you, too," said Brendan.

"You were supposed to be here fifteen minutes ago."

"Well, I'm here now, aren't I?"

"What'd you say?"

"You heard me."

Everyone at the table stopped what they were doing. They all turned to Ducie and waited for his reaction.

"Listen to this motherfucker," said Ducie. "He does a three-spot at Rikers and comes out talking gangster. Is that from all the black dick you had in your mouth?"

Everyone at the table laughed.

"You wish," said Brendan.

Ducie lit a cigarette and grinned.

After a moment, a waitress approached their table with coffee.

They took a van to the long-term parking lot at LaGuardia. After parking on a side street a few blocks from the entrance, they got out and made their way to the lot, carrying black duffel bags filled with Glock 19 pistols with the serial numbers scratched off, sawed-off Mossberg 590 Persuader pump-action shotguns, portable oxy-acetylene torch kits, and high-speed industrial angle grinders. The planes flew lower and lower the closer they got to the airport, and the collective sound of their engines grew louder all around them.

They headed toward the row of cars farthest from the entrance. Brendan stepped forward from the group and pulled an eighteen-inch slim jim from his waistband. While the others stood lookout, he approached an older Ford F-150 and looked inside. Seeing the blinking red LED light of a car alarm underneath the dashboard, he backed off and looked around for another older-looking truck.

He spotted a blue 1988 Dodge Ram with Vermont plates in the next row. He approached. There were no LED lights or stickers on the windows, nor any other telltale signs of a car alarm. He bumped the truck with his rear end to trigger any hidden alarms, then slipped the hooked end of the slim jim between the driver's side window and its rubber seal.

A few of the others turned to watch. Brendan worked with the grace and efficiency of a vaudevillian escape artist on stage. No stranger to stealing cars, in many ways he was even a natural at it. Some were good at driving, like Tommy. Others were good at fighting, like Sean and Whale. Some were good at giving orders, like Ducie, and others were good at taking them, like J.J. But Brendan was good at getting into things: cars, houses, safes. Within seconds, he managed to catch the rods connecting to the door's lock mechanism, and once that was done, he quickly unlocked and opened the door.

He slid in behind the wheel and pulled a short flathead screwdriver out of his back pocket. Then he jammed it into the lock and broke open the steering column. He quickly found the ignition wires, connected them, and started the engine. The entire process took less than thirty seconds.

Brendan got out of the truck. Ducie shoved past him,

nearly knocking him over. He tossed a duffel bag onto the empty passenger seat, got in, and drove off without saying a word.

Brendan approached an older Chevy pickup and went to work on it. Forty seconds later, he had the engine started. After he got out, Whale took his place behind the wheel, taking another one of the duffel bags with him. He dropped the truck's transmission into gear and drove off after Ducie.

Brendan glanced around the lot for one last vehicle, something with enough seats for the rest of them. He spotted a rust-eaten Dodge Caravan in the next row with a faded WILTON HIGH SCHOOL SOCCER sticker peeling and bubbling across its corroded bumper. He popped its driver's side door lock with the slim jim, got in, and went to work on the ignition. He found the right wires and touched them together, and the minivan's engine coughed and sputtered to life.

They took the Long Island Expressway east in the direction of Patchogue. Sean sat in the passenger's seat next to Tommy and went through the CD holder he had found behind the overhead visor. Brendan and J.J. sat in back. A few cars were heading west toward the city on the opposite side of the highway, but hardly any traffic headed east at that hour.

"Son of a bitch," said Sean.

"What?"

"There's nothing here but Air Supply and Linda Ronstadt."

"So?"

"So couldn't we have stolen something with better music? How the fuck am I supposed to get up to this shit?"

"Put on K-Rock," said J.J.

"K-Rock sucks," said Sean, continuing to thumb through the visor full of CDs. "I want to hear something dope, like some Nas or some Wu-Tang Clan."

"Would you just shut the fuck up?" said Tommy. "We've got a job to do here. Put your game face on."

They rode on in silence. After they passed West Islip, J.J. opened one of the duffel bags and handed out military-grade Kevlar vests and latex gloves. Just before noon, they came up on a black-and-red armored car. Ducie went on ahead of them in the Dodge and passed the armored piggy bank; Whale went on ahead of them in the Chevy.

Two miles later, an orange DETOUR sign appeared in the distance off to the side of the road. The armored car began to slow as it approached the sign. After a moment, a cell phone rang. Tommy answered before turning to the others.

"We're on," he said.

J.J. handed out pistols and Sesame Street Halloween masks. He gave Sean an orange Ernie mask and kept a yellow Bert for himself. Then he gave a blue Cookie Monster to Tommy and a green Oscar the Grouch to Brendan. The smirking, trashcan-lid-topped face made Brendan's stomach turn.

The armored car soon turned off for the detour. Tommy followed from a distance. After another mile, the Chevy that Whale had been driving jackknifed across the road just ahead of an intersection. To still his trembling fingers, Brendan wrapped them tightly around the grip of his pistol.

The armored car slowed as it approached the parked Chevy. As soon as it reached the intersection, the Dodge came barreling toward the intersection from the road to their right, still accelerating as it approached. Before the driver of the armored car could react, the Dodge T-boned it in a crunching explosion of steel and glass, lifting it up off the ground. The impact accordioned the front of the Dodge and set off its airbags, and the armored car balanced precariously on two wheels for a moment before tipping over and slamming down onto its side.

Everything fell silent for a few seconds. Then the driver's side door of the Dodge creaked as Ducie forced it open. He crawled out of the crumpled cab, a pistol in one hand and a red Elmo mask covering his face. Whale jogged toward the scene brandishing a shotgun and wearing a bright yellow Big Bird mask. Tommy pulled the minivan within twenty feet of the armored car and skidded it to a fishtailing stop, its tires squealing. The others threw open their doors and jumped out, rushing toward the armored car with their masks on and their pistols and shotguns drawn.

Brendan grabbed an oxy-acetylene torch kit and an angle grinder and hurried after the others, his heart hammering. J.J. tossed another duffel bag to Ducie, and when he reached the armored car, Ducie rapped against the windshield with the butt of his pistol.

"Get out," he shouted.

The chubby driver didn't move. Neither did the other guard, a gray-haired man old enough to be one of their fathers. Ducie pulled a stick of construction-grade dynamite from the duffel bag and waved it in front of the windshield.

"Get the fuck out," he shouted. "Now."

The driver held up his hands as he struggled toward the door. He fumbled to unlock it and then pushed it open. Ducie yanked him from the cab and took his pistol from him, and the driver promptly vomited onto Ducie's shoes.

"Motherfucker," said Ducie.

He shoved the driver toward the back of the armored car.

"Move," he said.

Tommy pulled the other guard from the cab and pushed him after the others. They all gathered around the back of the armored car.

"Open it," said Ducie.

"We can't—"

Ducie broke the driver's nose with the butt of his pistol, then put the pistol to the man's temple.

"Open the fucking door," shouted Ducie. "Now."

"We don't have a key," said the older guard. "Even if we did, it automatically locks after an accident."

Brendan stepped forward with the oxy-acetylene torch kit and put a pair of goggles over his mask. He lit the torch and began cutting through the armored car's back door.

"Hurry," said Ducie.

The others watched impatiently as the white-hot flame chewed its way through the metal. Brendan continued until he cut a crude black circle around the lock. The process took him no longer than it took to steal a car.

"Done," he said.

Tommy put on a work glove and stepped forward as Brendan backed away from the door. He used the butt of his shotgun to punch in the cut circle of metal. Then he reached into the hole that it left behind and pulled open the door.

As soon as he did, a shotgun blast exploded from inside the back of the armored car, knocking him backward and off his feet. Brendan and the others scattered as a third guard inside the back of the armored car fired at them again. The blast briefly illuminated the back of the armored car and echoed off its thick steel walls. Part of the shot hit Brendan in the chest and knocked him onto his back. He hit the ground, sucking for air. When he reached up for his chest, he half-expected to find a hole there, but his fingers found the body armor still in place, though savaged by the shot spread.

Ducie and Whale emptied their pistols into the back of the armored car. Nearby, the older guard dove for the ground. One of the bullets fired by Whale tore through the throat of the driver just above his bulletproof vest. The driver fell to his knees, wheezing and clutching as blood shot out from his jugular in a bright red spray. The guard in the back of the armored car fired one more time at them before Ducie and Whale could empty their clips into him.

The guard's final shotgun blast peppered Whale's bulletproof vest and the sleeve of his jacket; he stumbled when another shot rang out nearby and hit one of his legs. Brendan spun around. The older guard crouched on the ground, pointing Tommy's pistol at Whale. Brendan raised his own pistol and leveled it at the older man, but he hesitated. The guy reminded him of Richie. Before the older guard could fire again, a bullet struck his arm, knocking the pistol loose, and two more shots hit him in the chest, knocking him backward. Brendan turned to watch Ducie fire one more shot into the man's face. Ducie then turned to face Brendan, who was still sitting there, frozen, with his pistol raised.

"What the fuck's the matter with you?" he said.

Sean spoke before Brendan could reply.

"Everyone all right?"

Ducie turned to Sean.

"Get the car," he said.

Sean jogged off toward the minivan. Ducie climbed into the back of the armored car. J.J. approached Tommy, who lay motionless on the ground, blood seeping through his shredded mask. Cookie Monster's bug-eyes and wavy, screwed-up grin looked hideous, completely out of place.

"Fuck," said J.J.

Brendan looked over to the area near Tommy, where the driver was bleeding out onto the pavement.

"We gotta get out of here," said Whale.

Carrying a large bag, Ducie climbed out of the back of the armored car. He fired a single shot into the back of the driver's head, splattering the pavement with a reddish-gray mess of brains and splintered skull.

"What the fuck did you do that for?" said J.J., tearing off his mask.

"No witnesses," said Ducie.

Sean pulled up in the minivan.

"Let's go," said Whale.

"Wait, what about Tommy?" asked J.J.

Ducie said nothing. With the dead guard's shotgun, he fired a shot at Tommy's right hand, pulverizing it. Then he pumped another shell into the chamber and fired it at Tommy's left hand, turning it to a pulp as well. He fired a third shot into Tommy's face, shattering what was left of his teeth.

"Jesus Christ," said J.J.

"Even God couldn't ID him now," said Ducie, wiping the shotgun's stock and trigger clean before dropping it to the ground.

They drove off. At the end of the block, Ducie opened the black bag and looked inside.

He frowned. "What the fuck is this?"

"What?" asked Sean.

Ducie pulled out a stack of banded ten-dollar bills.

"There isn't even a hundred grand in here," he said. "There was supposed to be a quarter of a million. This is bullshit."

Whale grunted his displeasure. Ducie shook his head

and shoved the money back into the bag. Brendan glanced back at the bodies scattered on the pavement in the intersection behind them.

CHAPTER FOUR

THEY took off their Kevlar vests and changed out of their clothes on the way back to Queens. Ducie counted the money twice before splitting it into five piles. They each received just over seventeen thousand dollars.

"What about Tommy?" asked Brendan.

"What about him?" said Sean.

"Shouldn't his mother get his share?"

"Are you fucking crazy?"

Brendan said nothing.

They left the minivan in an empty lot a few blocks from the Buccaneer. Ducie took a red two-and-a-half gallon poly can from the back of the minivan, unscrewed the lid, and began dousing the minivan with gasoline.

"Everyone lay low for a while," he said. "No seeing each other, no phone calls, no familiar places, no nothing. Understood?"

All nodded or consented through their silence. One by one, they peeled off and headed away in different directions. Brendan remained behind and watched as Ducie splashed the last of the gas over the minivan and tossed the empty can onto the back seat. Then he turned to Brendan, taking out his pack of cigarettes and shaking one loose.

"Well?" he said, lighting the cigarette and taking a drag. "What the fuck are you waiting for? We're done here."

Without waiting for a reply, Ducie flicked the burning cigarette into the minivan and walked away. Flames engulfed the seats, but Brendan did not stay to watch the fire spread. He walked off in the direction of the subway station at 90th and Elmhurst.

After a hundred yards, he glanced back at the burning minivan.

He hid the money—an unexpectedly small sheaf of bills no bigger than two slices of bread—inside one of the kitchen vents at the bakery and waited until Maureen left for her overnight shift before returning to their apartment. Although he took a long, hot shower before he went to bed, he could not sleep. In his mind, the armored car guard kept going down, dark flowers of blood blossoming on the man's chest. And Tommy's face. The shotgun blast kept turning it into raw hamburger.

Brendan was still awake when the alarm went off, so he got up, showered again, and went to the bakery.

He put in an order with Nicky, promising to pay him in cash. He had thought it would feel good to restock his supplies, to get the business going again, but it did not.

It was worse than before. Much worse.

For three days and three nights, Brendan didn't see Maureen. Every morning, he left before she got home from the hospital; every evening, he worked late. By the time he got back from the bakery, she was already gone.

The fourth night after the robbery, when Brendan got home, he found Maureen there—even though she was supposed to be at work. Eyes puffy and red from crying, she was shoving her things into two suitcases and a pair of garbage bags.

"What are you doing?" he asked.

She responded without looking up from her packing: "I just talked to my Aunt Maggie."

"So?"

"So Tommy's missing."

"What's that got to do with me?"

"You're the last person who called him. Maggie saw your fucking number on his cell."

Her words hit him like a punch in the gut. After a moment, Maureen spoke again: "You know, the funny thing is, I don't even want to know what happened to him. That probably sounds fucked-up, but it's true."

He approached her.

"Baby—"

She shoved him away.

"*Don't you fucking touch me!*" she shouted.

He backed off.

"I'm done," she said. "I told you I'm not gonna end up like my mother and grow old waiting for you while you rot in prison."

She grabbed the suitcases and the garbage bags and pushed past him on her way toward the door.

"Maureen, wait—"

"Have a nice life."

She slammed the door behind her. He stood there for a long moment, then looked over at the wall.

She had left all of the photographs of them behind.

Brendan woke with a start the next day when an ambulance screamed past his building. His skull throbbed, and it was difficult to tell where the buzzing in his head ended and where the noise from the ambulance began. He was on the floor. One of his shoes was off, and the other was still on his foot, though the laces were untied. Spots on his chef pants looked like dried blood. Bile stung the back of his throat.

He glanced around the apartment, piecing together a fractured narrative of the night before: empty fifth of vodka, white pills—Vicodin, maybe. He couldn't remember where he had gotten them, what they were, or even how many he had taken. Broken glass sparkled on the floor. All of the picture frames had been smashed. He looked at the knuckles of his right hand. All but one were cut up and scabbed with dried blood. He tried to make a fist and screamed in surprised pain: his index and middle fingers felt broken.

He struggled to his feet and staggered toward the door. His knees buckled, and the floor tilted beneath him. Then he stopped. The DVD player displayed the time, 4:00 PM, too late to go in.

He braced himself against the wall for a moment before pitching toward the bathroom, and when he finally reached the sink, he puked. After he finished throwing up, he went back out into the living room. The television was still on, some program about China on CNN. Sean was always talking about how great China was, how great his cousins were doing, and how everything was there for the taking, like it was the Wild West.

"China," Brendan said aloud, his voice sounding very distant, his throat thick with foul, stinging phlegm.

Brendan showered and put on some clean clothes. After choking down some cold, day-old coffee, he left his apartment and went to the library. He looked into the entry requirements for China and found out that he'd need a visa for the mainland but not for Hong Kong. But there was a hitch. He was still on parole. If he left the country, a parolee-at-large warrant would be issued for his arrest.

But if he *didn't* leave the country… well, there was no way he was going back to prison.

Brendan began the process of shutting down the bakery. He sold the convection oven to a restaurant-supply store over on the Lower East Side, on Delancey Street. He only got half of what he had originally paid, but half was better than nothing. He sold the rest of his things to a consignment store in Jackson Heights, and whatever he couldn't sell, he left at the curb outside the Salvation Army.

On an afternoon soon after pawning off the trappings of his old life, he took the subway out to Far Rockaway. After he got off the train, he walked four blocks to the street where his Aunt Theresa lived. As a boy, more than a decade ago, he had been there with his mother, so he vaguely remembered the location and layout of the house. For a while, his aunt had tried to help him after his mother had died, but she had given up after his second trip to Tyron. They had not spoken since.

A rust-eaten van was parked in the driveway outside their small, rundown brick house. He waited at a bus stop at the end of the block for an hour until Theresa came out of the front door with her twenty-six-year-old son John, who looked like Brendan—except for the condition his body was in. He suffered from severe cerebral palsy and was confined to a wheelchair. Seeing his cousin from a distance sent that childhood punch of sadness through his chest. He vaguely wished he could be different for his family, but he had done enough bad things, and been in enough bad places, to have gotten over the worst phases of remorse and guilt.

Theresa loaded John's chair into the van, got in, and backed it up. As soon as they drove off, Brendan approached the house and broke in through the cellar door. The cheap tumbler lock was no match for him. Once inside, he made his way to an office on the second floor.

Brendan didn't find what he was looking for in the filing cabinet, but he found a cheap little security safe under a pile of folded winter clothes in the closet. He used a car pick to unlock it, and he had it open in a matter of seconds. Inside the safe, he found John's passport, along with John's and Theresa's birth certificates and Social Security cards.

Brendan looked at the photograph inside the passport.

He could pass for his cousin, at least in a one-inch-by-one-inch photograph that only showed him from the neck up. Besides, there was a chameleonic quality about him. People in their teens thought he was in his teens. Twenty-somethings thought he was in his twenties, and people in their thirties thought he was their age, too. He looked like a Brendan, but he also looked like a Danny, or a Kevin, or a Michael, or even a John, or a John Henry Davis, as it stated in his cousin's passport. *Tabula rasa*—he remembered the phrase from one of his classes at P.S. 70 before he had gotten shipped off to Tryon. That was him, a *tabula rasa*. It wasn't just easy for him to get into cars and houses and safes. It was easy for him to get into other identities as well. Athlete. Burnout. Model prisoner. Baker. Thief. One difficult part was staying in a particular role. The other difficult part was wondering half the time just who the hell he was.

Brendan flipped through the pages of the passport. There were only two stamps inside: one from France, five years before, and the other from US immigration a week after that. John would not need it any time soon, Brendan figured. So he wouldn't notice that it was gone, either.

After slipping John's passport into his pocket, Brendan locked the safe and put it back where he had found it. Downstairs, he stopped over a stack of old photo albums on a shelf in the living room. He hesitated, then went over to look through them, doubtful he would find any pictures of his mother or himself. But inside the second album, a few faded photographs depicted him and his parents at a picnic. He was maybe two years old. There was one of his

young father, rolling an inflatable beach ball to him. A lit
cigarette dangled from his father's mouth, and crude sailor
tattoos peeked out from underneath the sleeves of his white
t-shirt. There was another one of him sitting in his teenage
mother's lap at a picnic table, sharing a plate of what looked
like macaroni salad. Brendan remembered none of it. In
all the pictures, they were smiling, and they looked happy.
This must have been a year or two before his father had left,
maybe three or four years before his mother had begun her
descent into the black waters of heroin. It was like looking
at pictures of someone else, pictures of strangers. Even his
own smiling face was hard for him to recognize.

Brendan put the album back on the shelf, regretting
that he had looked. The last thing he needed was to ques-
tion his resolve. He left the house through the cellar door
and locked it behind him.

He bought a round-trip ticket from JFK to Hong Kong
International Airport on a Cathay Pacific Airways flight.
Packing did not take long; he did not have that much, just
a few changes of clothing, a leather toiletry kit, and the
tattered copy of *The Tassajara Bread Book* that Richie had
given him, all of which fit into his faded Mets duffel bag.
He also had about $25,000 in cash, which he taped to his
stomach with cellophane wrap. After he put on a baggy
sweatshirt, the money was impossible for anyone to see.

He wrote a letter to Maureen before leaving for the
airport. He wrote three of them, actually. In the first letter,

he tried to explain himself to her. He tore it up after reading it. The second letter was a long and drawn-out apology for all the mistakes that he'd made. He tore that one up before he'd even finished writing it. The last letter he wrote contained only five words—*I'm sorry* and *You deserve better*—along with seventy-five hundred dollars, which he knew she needed for nursing school tuition and for her rusty Honda Accord. But he didn't send the letter because he knew she wouldn't keep it. She would return it to the police. So he tore up the last letter and taped the additional cash to his stomach with the rest of the money.

He took the A train to the Howard Beach station and caught the shuttle to the airport from there. He went through security without a hitch and found his gate. While waiting for the boarding announcement, he looked at the latest editions of *The New York Times, The Daily News,* and *The Post.* The robbery was not mentioned in any of them. At first, he was relieved, but that didn't cancel out that final phone call he had made to Tommy. That sent his heart skipping again, and he felt sick once more.

On board, he found his window seat next to a middle-aged Chinese businessman. Not long after buckling in, he began to get nervous. They were on the tarmac for a long time, and he wondered if someone had recognized him, or if Theresa had noticed that John's passport was missing, or if one of the others had gotten caught and turned him in. It was the first time that he had ever been on a plane, and he was starting to feel as if he was back in a cell at Rikers. His chest tightened and his heart began to race, and he wished he'd brought a few Xanax with him.

He closed his eyes and leaned back in his seat. After a moment, he heard Tommy's voice.

"What the fuck are you doing?"

Brendan opened his eyes and saw Tommy sitting in the seat next to him where the Chinese businessman had been, two stumps where his hands once were and blood seeping through the tattered Cookie Monster mask.

"What the hell do you know about China, other than some shit you saw in a movie?" said Tommy. "You don't actually think you're going to get away with this, do you?"

Brendan said nothing.

"This is a bad idea," said Tommy. "I hate to piss on your little parade here, but people don't change. The shit will follow you. I guarantee it."

Brendan closed his eyes again and tightly gripped the handles of the seat. He blocked everything out and waited.

After a long moment, the captain's voice came over the intercom.

"Cabin crew, please prepare for take-off."

Brendan opened his eyes. The Chinese businessman was once again sitting in the seat next to him, reading a copy of *The Hong Kong Economic Times*. Tommy was nowhere to be seen.

He looked ahead to the seatback in front of him. Before long, the plane finally began to taxi toward the runway, and after its massive engines rumbled and shook, it took off and rose above the city.

Once they reached a cruising altitude, Brendan looked out the window and glanced back in the direction that they had come from.

Everything looked so different from thirty thousand feet.

CHAPTER FIVE

SHANGHAI, CHINA
TWELVE YEARS LATER

THE alarm went off at three-thirty. It was set to some Cantopop tune on Li's MP3 player, Hotcha or at17, one of the girl bands Xiaodan was learning how to dance to.

Brendan reached out and shut off the music before it got halfway through the chorus. Then he glanced over at Li and watched her shift beneath the sheets. She looked so beautiful there, so peaceful and relaxed. He'd fallen for her the moment he first saw her, about six months after he'd arrived in Hong Kong. She had been sitting at a table in a crowded *chaa chan teng*, studying a dog-eared English textbook. She was nineteen years old, but she looked older. She had caught him staring at her, but instead of getting angry or shying away from his gaze, she'd confidently held it. With that, he was hooked. She'd fallen quickly for him as well, or at least fallen for who she thought he was—John Henry Davis, former merchant marine and recent culinary school graduate from Long Island looking to start over and open a bakery somewhere in Asia, maybe somewhere a bit cheaper and less developed than Hong Kong. He was older, better looking, and more interesting than the delivery boys who chased after her, or the boring laundry shop and noodle-bar managers her mother tried to set her up with. Like many Chinese relationships, there was a transactional nature to it: for her, he had been a way out of a world she wanted to exit, and for him, she had been a way into one.

After watching her sleep for a moment, Brendan got up and went to put on some coffee. The scuffed wooden floor of their apartment was cold beneath his bare feet. In a few months it would be spring again, and it would be warm and humid, but for now, the bitter Shanghainese winter prevailed.

He dropped to the floor and knocked out a few hundred push-ups while waiting for the coffee to brew. Even though he was in his late thirties, he was in better shape than he'd been in his mid-twenties, when he'd left New York. He stayed fit and he ate moderately. He didn't smoke, drink, or use drugs, but he didn't do these things out of virtue—he did them out of necessity. He would have loved to have just one or two drinks or maybe a few OxyContin every now and then—which were cheaply and readily available on every street corner in Shanghai without the need for a prescription—but he never had just one or two, or even eight or nine, so he left it alone.

The coffee was ready by the time he finished his push-ups. After he poured himself a cup, he began preparing breakfast for Xiaodan. He cut up a pair of small yellow mangoes he'd gotten from a wet market and dropped the pieces into a bowl, then put some rice and water into the cooker and turned it on so it would become congee by the time they woke.

Once he finished making breakfast, Brendan grabbed a t-shirt and a pair of jeans off the clothes rack and pulled them on. Then he went in and looked at Xiaodan in her crib. She lay there with her knees bent and her rear end pointing up toward the ceiling as if in *sasangasana*, the rabbit pose. She looked adorable; he could have stood there all day, taking her in. Before she had come into the world, he thought astrology and anything related to it was a joke, something for new agers and hippies, or pick-up line fodder—but he was no longer so sure. Born under the same zodiac sign he was, three full cycles later, like him she was unpredictable, rebellious, daring, and impulsive, even at two years old. She was also restless, impatient, quick-tempered, and obstinate like him, though he worked hard to keep those emotions in check. He was proud and glad she took after him, but he was also afraid for her, and he hoped she wouldn't take on all of his traits or end up following a path similar to his.

He carefully draped the blanket back over her and quietly exited the room. Then he pulled on a hooded sweatshirt and leather jacket and left the apartment. Outside, it was still dark, and a light mist was falling. The rain cleared the smog from the air, but it made all other smells come out and into sharp focus: the pools of coagulating grease around trashcans and behind restaurants, the diesel fumes, the pollen from the buds of the birch trees and the ginkgos and the London planes. The dog shit and the chemicals from the recently painted buildings. Like the New York City he'd left behind, Shanghai was a cornucopia of smells, and its own particular scent was as distinct as a brand of aftershave or perfume.

He left through the gate and went out into the narrow lane. Compared to the gleaming skyscrapers surrounding it, their apartment building was practically invisible. As with so much of the old city, it was concealed and hidden within a maze of high walls topped with barbed wire and shards of broken glass. Though the *lilongs* and *shíkùmén*-style buildings were being razed and replaced by high-rise commercial developments and condos every day, hundreds of lanes just like it existed in Shanghai's former French Concession, which made it a great place for hiding out or getting lost.

He walked north toward Nanjing Lu and Tomorrow City. Like many things in Shanghai and China, Tomorrow City was a bit of a sham, little more than a hastily built group of generic-looking buildings surrounding a small and forgettable park. None of the guidebooks even bothered to mention it, and it didn't have the history or allure of Beijing's Forbidden City or Hong Kong's Walled City—but that was the point. Brendan could hide his bakery in plain sight and still do good business; it wasn't so remote that he couldn't make a living, but it wasn't so trafficked by tourists that he might risk getting spotted, either.

He listened to a mix on his MP3 player as he made his way to the bakery: Jane's Addiction, The Clash, Black Flag, and other songs from his youth. On the sidewalks around him, a few expats stumbled home from drunken nights out while some early-rising migrants raked through trashcans for empty bottles. On Fuxing Lu over by the embassies, a group of fresh-faced Chinese soldiers replaced a tired-looking unit whose shift was coming to an end, and a lone billsticker pasted up a red-and-gold poster, the first of what would be many in the weeks leading up to the Lunar New Year celebration. Other than that, the streets were empty. They were his; it was his favorite time of day, when anything seemed possible.

By the time Brendan got to the bakery, it was just before four o'clock. He'd recently added an expansion and had begun a sit-down service to go along with the takeaway they did, so his days were beginning earlier and earlier. Hamilton was already there, waiting for him by the back entrance. A gangly teen from the Anhui countryside, Hamilton had chosen his English name from an old British textbook. Brendan had thought about telling him how outdated the name Hamilton was, but the boy loved it, and Brendan didn't want to hurt the guy's feelings. Besides, he could've picked something worse. Since moving to China, Brendan had met plenty of Jolies, Protons, Cruises, and Fish. He'd even met a guy named Cheddar once. At least Hamilton wasn't a flavor or the surname of a Hollywood celebrity.

Hamilton looked up and smiled as Brendan approached.

"Good morning, sir," he said.

"Morning," said Brendan.

They went inside. Hamilton took out the supplies while Brendan fired up his Blodgett Zephaire double-deck gas convection oven. It was a beautiful piece of equipment: six feet high and thirteen hundred pounds of gleaming stainless steel, with dual-pane thermal-glass windows encased in the oven door frames, five chrome-plated racks in each oven, and double-sided porcelainized baking compartment liners inside. And it wasn't all just show, either—it pumped out 120,000 BTUs and could churn out enough bread every day to feed a small village. Brendan had purchased it seven years before at an auction from another Westerner whose business had failed, and though it had been much more than he could afford at the time, he had never once regretted buying it.

After he got the oven preheating, Brendan began working on his dough. Though he could've saved himself time and effort and used a straight dough made in one step, he preferred to pre-ferment as Richie had taught him. He also preferred to produce his own yeast rather than use the commercially produced form. Doing these extra things cost more time and money, but they made the bread more flavorful and gave it a better texture.

By four-thirty, Brendan and Hamilton were shaping loaves and filling muffin and bread pans with batter. By five o'clock, they started loading things into the oven. The air grew thick with the yeasty, earthy scent of baking bread. Brendan glazed the cooling doughnuts or filled them with jelly or cream for the expats or red-bean paste for the locals; Hamilton brewed massive urns of coffee and squeezed fresh juices from oranges and beets. At five-thirty, a local seventeen-year-old girl named Jessie showed up to work the cash register out front, and at six o'clock, she unlocked the front door.

Brendan spent the entire morning in the kitchen as he usually did. It wasn't just to keep out of view, either—he loved it back there. In the kitchen, things were timeless and perfect. He was a little boy standing back in his grandparents' kitchen watching his mother make French toast, before things had gotten bad, and he was in his late thirties in his own kitchen, and he was every age in between. He was in Queens, and he was in Shanghai, and yet he was nowhere and everywhere at the same time. There was no past and no future but only the present, and in the present, there was bread to be made. As soon as something was taken out of the oven, something else went in; as soon as one batter or dough was used, another was made. When it was all finished, there were things to be cleaned and prepared for the following day. The time flew by, and it always surprised him when the afternoon rolled around.

At one o'clock, Brendan left Hamilton and Jessie in charge and went back to his apartment. The aroma of steaming *baozi* greeted him as he opened the front door. He approached Li, who was over at the sink, washing dishes.

"Hey, babe," he said, kissing her.

"Hey," she replied.

He glanced around the apartment.

"She still asleep?" he asked.

Li nodded. "Busy morning," she said. "She didn't want to leave the playground."

Brendan went to Xiaodan's room and found her there, sitting up in her crib and rubbing the sleep from her eyes. She looked up at him and smiled.

"*Bàba*," she said.

He picked her up from her bed and brought her over to the changing table. Unlike the Chinese, they used diapers rather than slit pants. After he finished changing her, he brought Xiaodan out into the other room and put on her bib. Then he put her down at the table, and she ate seven of the *baozi*. She had an appetite like a horse, but where she'd gotten it was a mystery to them both.

They went to the park after they finished eating; a number of locals were there, performing *qigong* exercises. An older man slapped the sides of a tree with his bare arms and grunted, and two couples practiced ballroom dancing to some tinny music playing on a boombox.

Just after four o'clock, the sun went down behind a thick veil of smog and clouds. There was only one time zone for all of China and no daylight saving time, so the winter days grew dark early in Shanghai. They left the park and walked over to Yuen's apartment for afternoon tea. A few years after retiring from the tailor's shop where she had worked, Yuen had followed her daughter from Hong Kong to Shanghai, and she lived in a small one-bedroom apartment a few blocks from theirs. Unlike most Chinese parents who lived with their adult children, she preferred her autonomy. Brendan didn't mind in the least, as he preferred his own autonomy as well.

They sat at a table in Yuen's cramped apartment and sipped weak *chá* from mismatched porcelain cups. While Xiaodan played on the floor with some handmade wooden blocks, Yuen spoke to Li. Her heavy Cantonese dialect was impossible for Brendan to understand; it sounded so flat and choppy compared to Mandarin or the lilting and singsongy Shanghainese, and everything blurred together as if Yuen were talking through a mouthful of food. It was as foreign to Brendan as Greek, which was clearly Yuen's reason for speaking it around him. Even to an outsider, it was obvious by the way she looked at him and spoke to him that she didn't like him: he was just another *gweilo*, a ghost man, a foreign devil there to take from them and to bring mayhem and destruction. He felt as if she could somehow see inside him and read his thoughts, and he never felt comfortable around her.

He left them just before five o'clock and went back to the bakery to make dough for the next day. And as he did every evening, he took the items that hadn't been sold out back to give away to the poor. Fang and Wei were there, two women in their fifties who lived in one of the crumbling lane houses in the shadows of the Tomorrow Square tower. They'd been friends since childhood, and they had grown up in a Shanghai that was unrecognizable from the Shanghai of the present. With them was a homeless man in his sixties named Wuyi who spent his days in the park. Brendan didn't recognize the other two people, but he knew word got around, and he preferred giving away the old bread rather than throwing it out. Judging by their homemade shoes and crooked yellow teeth, he assumed they were recently arrived migrant workers from somewhere out in the countryside. Maybe Anhui, he thought, or Heilongjiang. The city was full of them, and thousands more arrived every day.

"*Ni hao*," said Brendan.

"*Ni hao*," they all replied.

"Today weather nice," he said.

They smiled at his broken Shanghainese.

"The weather is nice," one of the women said back to him in Shanghainese, speaking slowly enough for him to understand. "Maybe spring will be here soon."

It was a good day in terms of business, and there wasn't much left to give away. Brendan's muffins had sold out again, and so did his doughnuts. The scones weren't selling well, and he made a mental note to cut back on them. There were a couple of loaves of sourdough left, but it was normally in demand and he didn't anticipate it becoming a trend. He wanted to bring a loaf of it home for Li and Xiaodan anyway; Xiaodan had a few molars coming in, and its chewy crusts would be good for her gums.

The back door to the bakery swung open.

"Sir?"

Brendan looked over to see Hamilton standing in the doorway.

"There's some reporter here," Hamilton said. "White lady."

"What does she want?"

"She says she wants to run a story about the expansion. For *Shanghai Family* or something."

"Take care of it, will you?"

"You sure?"

Brendan nodded as he continued handing out the bread.

Hamilton went back inside. Somewhere in the distance,

a roving scrap merchant pedaled past on his bicycle-drawn cart, ringing a makeshift bell.

After closing the bakery, Brendan took a taxi to the strip of electronics stores in Xujiahui to pick up a new blender. On his way back to the apartment, he bought some flowers for Li from one of the wet markets on Wulumuqi Lu.

The apartment was empty when he got there. He put the flowers in a vase and filled it with water, sat down, and checked his email. There were a few messages from his suppliers: the price of flour was going up; another supplier asked if the time of the milk delivery could be changed. There was some typo-filled spam from a new massage parlor on Nanjing Xi Lu that was offering "half-prize messages." There was also an email from Hamilton that said GOOD NEWS in the subject line and had a link to the website of a local magazine.

Brendan clicked on the link and watched as a new window opened on his screen. His heart stopped when he saw a photo of himself standing behind the counter of the bakery.

CHAPTER SIX

THEY entered the bakery through the back door, carrying sacks of flour and crates of brown eggs smeared with dried albumen and dirt.

"What the hell were you thinking?" asked Brendan.

"I beg your pardon?" said Hamilton.

"How'd she get my picture?"

"She asked for it."

"When did you take it?"

"I don't remember," said Hamilton. "Sometime last year, I think. Jessie took it."

"I thought I told you guys no pictures?"

"I thought you'd be happy, sir. It's free advertising, isn't it?"

Before Brendan could reply, his cell phone rang. He glanced at its display.

"Did I do something wrong?" asked Hamilton.

"Just get the bread in the oven," said Brendan.

Hamilton stared blankly at Brendan as he walked off and took the call.

The day was a long, slow train wreck. The great thing about doing business in China was that there were few barriers to entry, few regulations, and runaway growth. The difficult thing about doing business in China was there were few barriers to entry, few regulations, and runaway growth. Suppliers with no experience or track record often delivered products from suspect sources, products past their expiration dates, or products that were clearly counterfeit or not what was promised. Entrepreneurs entered business overnight and closed just as quickly. Workers were easy to find, but hard to train and even harder to keep; people left without warning as soon as better opportunities presented themselves. Language was also a major obstacle: Brendan's Shanghainese was good, but it was far from perfect; as good as the English of his employees and suppliers was, it was also very flawed. Orders and instructions and arrangements usually worked out, but they were rarely exact, and much got lost in translation.

They'd lost another supplier before opening. Most of their butter went rancid, and they had to buy more from an expensive supermarket at the nearby Kerry Center. Brendan lost Hamilton for four hours to take care of these things, and the girl who normally helped Jessie in the afternoon never showed up, but they sold nearly everything they'd baked, and they'd even gotten another large catering order for an upcoming gallery opening. Even when business was bad in China, it was still much better than it ever would have been back in Queens.

Brendan stayed late to prepare for the following day. On his way home, he stopped to get some fruit for Xiaodan. By the time he got back to their apartment, Xiaodan was already asleep. He went into her room and kissed her on the forehead, then left her door half open and made his way back to the bedroom.

Li was already in bed; she had fallen asleep reading again. This time, it was T. Colin Campbell's *The China Diet*. A tall stack of books towered on the night table next to her. She was usually reading a dozen different things at once— books on business and investing, diet and health, computer programming, child rearing, advanced English. Like so many other young and upwardly mobile Chinese, she was always looking to improve herself and get ahead, and there wasn't a single volume of fiction or anything remotely entertaining or impractical in the entire stack.

Brendan shucked off his clothes and crawled into bed. He didn't even bother to brush his teeth, and he fell asleep soon after closing his eyes.

In his dreams, he found himself running, and when he looked back to see what was chasing him, he saw Ducie smiling a blood-soaked grin.

CHAPTER SEVEN

BRENDAN glanced at the alarm clock. It read 2:18 AM in harsh neon-red numbers. He rolled over and closed his eyes, but he couldn't fall back asleep.

For days, he found himself worrying about Ducie. He saw Ducie in the faces of strangers he passed on the street, and he saw Ducie in the customers who came into the bakery. He thought about him whenever he looked at Li and Xiaodan; he even dreamed about Ducie chasing him through Shanghai's back alleys and lanes.

Though nothing had yet come of it, Brendan considered the matter far from closed. If any of his old set came looking for him, he was vulnerable. As a witness to a job that had gone wrong and left four dead, he couldn't afford to assume the matter closed just because twelve years had passed. During the years that Brendan had known him, Ducie had never let anything go. After getting out of Tryon, Ducie had killed a guard who'd been hard on him. Another time, they had run into a man at a highway rest stop who owed Ducie fifty dollars on a bet they'd made during the 1995 NCAA Tournament. Ducie took everything the man had, including his gold necklace and car keys, then pummeled the guy with a broken mop handle and left him bleeding on the restroom floor with a broken jaw and separated shoulder.

While he lay there thinking about it, Brendan wondered if he should leave Shanghai. He wondered if he should pack up everything they had and take Li and Xiaodan back to Hong Kong, or on to Malaysia or Laos. But would they want to go with him? Would they be willing to leave her mother and everything they knew behind, as he'd done himself so many years before? And what about the bakery? He had put everything he owned into it. Would he be able to get any of it back? And more importantly, what about his passport? His cousin's had long since expired, and he was afraid to use the stolen Australian passport he'd bought a few years before from one of the Xinjiang drug dealers on Dongping Lu. He didn't know if it was even valid.

The only thing he ended up deciding was to put off the decision for a while. Until then, he'd look into his options. He would see if there were any interested parties in the bakery—there was always a steady supply of optimistic arrivals looking to make it big in China. He would also look into other countries and see what it would take to start over somewhere else. He had recently heard that Grenada was reinstating the passports-for-sale program it had offered in the nineties; maybe if he could get together enough money, he could buy one of those.

Brendan opened his eyes and looked back at the alarm clock. It read 2:23 AM. Only five minutes had passed since the last time he'd looked at it, but it felt as if hours had elapsed. He closed his eyes again and tried to think about something else—music, sex, even work. But nothing took his mind off things. So he thought about the vacation they'd taken the year before to Sanya, in the southern part of China. He thought about the constant grind of the moto-dups and the chattering macaques on Monkey Island; he thought of the endless golden beaches and the flowing casuarina trees that waved in the warm ocean breeze. But even that didn't work. So he thought about nothing at all. But thoughts of Ducie kept coming back to mind: thoughts of Ducie beating the guy at the highway rest stop, Ducie shooting the armored car guard in the face.

Brendan had rarely had trouble sleeping when he was young, even when he was at Rikers. And if he did, he'd just smoke a joint or take a Xanax or two and be out before he knew it. Even at Rikers, it had been easy to get drugs—but that was before he'd quit using. And that was before he'd met Li, and before she had Xiaodan. Now he had much more to lose, and he had nothing to take away the edge.

He thought of the Kurosawa film he'd recently watched with Li, *The Bad Sleep Well*. It hadn't really been his thing— he was more of an action fan, movies with Jason Statham or Chow Yun Fat. But one of the bootleg merchants in the neighborhood had all of the Criterion Collection DVDs for eight *kuài* each, and Li had bought a few of them. And after they'd watched it, something about the film had stuck with him, something about the way the protagonist couldn't sleep at the end after all the horrible things he had done. Did it mean he wasn't truly bad after all? Brendan wondered. Did it mean that deep down, he really had a conscience, despite all the things he'd done?

He continued to lie there for a while, but the more he thought about things, the more awake he became. Finally, he just shut off the alarm and got up. Then he went to do what he did whenever things were really bothering him and he couldn't get his mind to stop racing.

He put on his sneakers and went out for a run.

For Xiaodan's second birthday, Li and Yuen wanted to take her to the Shanghai Zoo. Since the photograph had been published online, Brendan had avoided going out in public other than to the bakery. But they'd been promising Xiaodan a trip to the zoo for months, and he didn't want to disappoint her, so on a Sunday afternoon, they all piled into a taxi and rode out to Nan Hui.

On the way, Xiaodan pointed out all the animals in an illustrated board book Li had purchased for her on Taobao. She was learning Mandarin and English at the same time, and she knew all of the animals' names in both languages: *xiàng* was elephant, *hóu* was monkey, *xióng* was bear, *hu* was tiger. Every time she named an animal, she looked up to Brendan to see if she was right, and every time he smiled and nodded to her, she beamed with pride.

They got to the zoo just after it had opened; the weak sun was struggling to shine through a thick blanket of haze and pollution. After paying the entrance fees, they set out. The winding grounds of the park covered an old golf course and reminded Brendan of the Bronx Zoo, though the conditions at Shanghai were much worse. It also reminded him of Rikers and Tryon somehow, dismal and institutional.

They meandered through the park. Xiaodan was too excited to ride in her stroller, so she ran on ahead of them with her stiff-legged and clumsy gait. She screamed and clapped when they saw the mandrills and spider monkeys; she hid behind Brendan's legs when they got to the polar bear cages. The panda bears didn't impress her, but she went hysterical over the kangaroos. Despite disliking zoos, Brendan couldn't help but vicariously feel some of her excitement and joy—he even forgot about the photograph for a while, and about Ducie, and about his past.

They spent all day covering the massive grounds of the park. At noon, they stopped for *cu miàn* and ice cream at an outdoor pagoda before continuing.

Late in the afternoon, they circled back toward the zoo's entrance. On their way, they approached a mixed group of Chinese and foreign tourists gathered around a fenced-in area, where a fully grown tiger slept against a concrete wall. A tour guide addressed the group in Mandarin first and then in English.

"Ladies and gentlemen, over here you'll see a South China tiger," he said. "*Panthera tigris amoyensis.* Also known as the Chinese, Amy, or Xiamen tiger. It is native to the forests of Southern China, and it is considered to be the 'stem' tiger or the subspecies from which all other tigers are descended."

The tour guide continued as the crowd looked on

and took photos of the animal with their cameras and smartphones.

"Like all other tigers, these animals are pure carnivores," he said. "They're expert hunters and will stalk their prey for hours. They kill with a bite to the back of the neck or use a suffocation hold on the throat. They can feed on almost anything, and they were known as man-eaters back when their population was higher."

One of the tourists threw a plastic water bottle at the tiger; it hit the tiger in the side, and the animal growled and swatted at the air. A few people oohed or aahed or laughed, but the majority seemed bored.

"It is also one of the ten most endangered animals in the world," said the tour guide. "In 1959, during the Great Leap Forward, the tiger and other predators were declared by the government to be pests and enemies of the people, and as a result, several anti-pest campaigns began. Although the decision was later reversed, experts maintain that there are fewer than twenty of these left in the wild, and they warn that it might become extinct within the next decade."

Brendan looked at the predator. It seemed old and tired, and nothing like the description the tour guide had given. Its eyes were red and inflamed; the fur on its chest was more yellow than white, and it hung down loosely like clothing that was two sizes too big. Then Brendan looked down at his left forearm, where there was a kidney-sized patch of skin lighter than the rest, where his tattoo used to be.

"Hate to say I told you so, but... I told you so."

Brendan looked up and saw Tommy standing near the

fence, still wearing the bloodied and shredded mask. His stumps were a mess of severed tendons, gristle, and splintered bone.

"You can't run away from things," said Tommy. "They always catch up with you."

Brendan said nothing.

"It's like that old story about the servant that rides to Samarra or wherever it was to escape death, only to end up finding death already there—"

Brendan interrupted him: "Nothing's gonna come of this," he said.

"If you really believed that, then you wouldn't be talking to me right now, would you?"

Brendan did not reply.

"Would you?" Tommy said again.

Brendan closed his eyes and took a deep breath. After a long moment, he heard Xiaodan shout nearby.

"*Bàba!*"

Brendan opened his eyes and looked over to see Xiaodan running and pointing toward the next penned-in area, where a number of ring-tailed lemurs swung from the branches of some plastic trees. Then he looked back over to the fence—Tommy was gone.

He moved on. After a few steps, he stopped and glanced back at the tiger.

It appeared to be looking in his direction, watching him go.

CHAPTER EIGHT

BRENDAN yanked open the upper door of the Blodgett Zephaire. A blast of hot air hit him in the face. He reached into the oven and pulled out a dozen fresh loaves of multi-grain bread, their high crowns ridged with cracked and golden peaks. After he set them aside to cool, he loaded in a few trays of uncooked scones.

He closed the oven door and wiped the sweat from his brow, then took a bowl down from a shelf and began dumping ingredients into it: sugar, vanilla extract, a few sticks of softened butter, a brick of cream cheese. He got out a blender and began whipping it all into a simple icing, then spooned the mixture into a pastry bag and iced some pumpkin muffins cooling on a nearby rack.

Almost a month had passed since his photograph had been published online. Brendan had finally started sleeping again, but the fear of Ducie showing up at any moment stayed with him. Ducie lurked in his thoughts like the smell of sulfur after a fireworks show: the more time that had elapsed, the more it went away, but it refused to disappear completely.

Once he was finished icing the muffins, Brendan took the scones from the oven and set them aside to cool. After he wiped his hands on his apron, he tossed it into a hamper full of dirty dishtowels, and he made his way out toward the front of the store.

Up front, Hamilton and Jessie were getting latte macchiatos and chocolate almond croissants for a pair of Western *tai tais* in expensive yoga outfits. Another customer sat at a table, sipping a cappuccino and picking at a muffin while scrolling through messages on a smartphone. A framed hundred-yuan note hung from the wall next to the cash register: Mao Zedong seemed to be stoically watching over everything from his vantage point on the front of the bill.

"How'd we do today?" asked Brendan.

"Good, sir," said Hamilton.

Brendan looked over the display case while Hamilton gathered the money from the register. It was nearly empty, which was rare for a Friday; everything had sold well, including the scones.

After Brendan took the money from Hamilton, he left through the back door and headed north. Outside, it was overcast and gray. A group of locals gathered at the outdoor market by the intersection of Wuyuan and Wulumuqi, haggling over the price of live prawns and sword beans. The ubiquitous Year of the Tiger decorations, the red Chinese knots, and hand-painted *duìlián* scrolls were everywhere, as it was only a day away from New Year's Eve. They filled storefronts and display windows, and they hung from doorways and rear-view mirrors.

He continued along Wulumuqi past a construction site by Anfu. A number of migrants were working there on the foundation of yet another new skyscraper. One welded with

a torch; not a single one of them wore glasses or protection. Showers of hot sparks fell on and around them as they
coupled together a pair of crossbeams. Nearby, someone lit
a string of firecrackers in an alleyway, startling Brendan. No
matter how many times he heard the sound of exploding
fireworks, he never got used to it, and he was dreading the
annual blitzkrieg that would be coming with the beginning
of the festivities.

He turned onto Anfu Lu and walked past the Western
boutiques and restaurants lining the street. At the end of the
block, he stopped at an ATM to deposit some of the money.
He no longer used the accounts he'd opened under John's
name—in fact, he'd stopped using them years before—and
instead used an account that Li had opened under her name.
The rest of his money he kept in cash along with the stolen
passport in his worn leather toiletry kit, hidden behind a
loose ceiling panel in his closet.

After he finished at the bank, he walked to Wukang
Lu and bought some cardamom at one of the wet markets
there. Then he headed back toward his apartment, passing
a few Westerners on his way. One wore a fitted suit and
looked like a business executive. Another carried a bag full
of books and papers and looked like an English teacher.
Most Westerners in Shanghai fell into one of those two
groups; for the most part, the area was still predominantly
Chinese. More and more expatriates arrived every year—
there were about a hundred and seventy five thousand out
of Shanghai's twenty-three million residents—but that
number included Japanese, Koreans, and other foreigners

as well. Someday there might be too many for him, but for now, he felt as if he could fly under the radar, especially if he stayed away from the touristy areas like Pudong and the Bund. It wasn't so Chinese that he stuck out, but it wasn't so Western that he felt that he fit in, either.

Li's bicycle was locked out front when he got back to the apartment building. Inside, a half-eaten bowl of noodles sat on the kitchen table. Brendan touched the side of the bowl—it was still warm.

"Li?" he said.

There was no reply.

"Anyone home?"

His chest tightened. He put down the market bag and went into Xiaodan's bedroom. Empty. He went into their bedroom next—also empty. He started to panic. Was it Ducie? he wondered. Could he really have found him? And if so, would he have taken Li and Xiaodan?

He hurried back toward the front door. Before he could get there, he heard something scuffling inside the closet underneath the stairs. He stopped and listened for a moment, then glanced around for a weapon, spotting a copper-bottomed pan hanging from a nail on the wall in the kitchen.

He crept back toward the closet, then raised the pan and flung open the door. His heart leapt into his throat as Xiaodan burst out from the darkness.

"Boo!"

She staggered around the room clapping and laughing. Li emerged from the shadows behind her.

"She heard you coming and wanted to scare you," she said.

Brendan looked at his daughter, who danced around the room. She'd recently learned the word *boo* and had taken to hiding behind chairs or under tables and jumping out and scaring him, but this was the first time she'd hidden in the closet.

Brendan hung the pan back on its nail, then stormed toward Xiaodan.

"I'm gonna get you!" he said.

Xiaodan laughed even harder. She ran away from him, cackling. He caught up to her and threw her over his shoulder, then tickled her underneath her tiny arms.

"How do you like that?" he said. "You think it's funny?"

Xiaodan laughed hysterically. So did Li.

Before long, even Brendan couldn't help but laugh as well.

They walked to the park on Huashan Lu, where Brendan and Xiaodan kicked a rubber ball back and forth until she wore herself out. They left when a thick wall of otherworldly yellow haze formed in the sky, a Shanghainese precursor to rain.

On their way back to the apartment, they stopped at a wet market to get some mangoes, but the seller had run out. Brendan promised he'd stop somewhere else after work, then dropped them off at home before heading back to the bakery.

Hamilton was out front when he got there, putting a loaf of bread into the slicer; Jessie had already left for the day. Brendan went back into the kitchen and began preparing dough for the following morning. He slid his MP3 player into a dock and put on some music, something to get him fired up and to take his mind off things. He chose The Stooges' *Fun House*, his favorite album. Then he whipped up some dough and batters as Iggy Pop's primal screaming came belting out over the speakers followed by Ron Asheton's blistering guitar.

He put everything into the walk-in refrigerator when he was finished and began cleaning up. Hamilton came back into the kitchen while he was doing the dishes; Brendan was listening to some Pavement to wind down after The Stooges album had ended.

"There's someone here to see you, sir," said Hamilton.

Brendan looked up from a sink full of suds. "Who is it?"

"I don't know," said Hamilton. "Big guy. *Lao hei*."

Brendan froze when he heard Hamilton say the local slang word for a black person. He shut off the water and quickly dried his hands, then went over to the door and peered through its small window. An enormous black man waited out front, standing by the counter, wearing cargo pants and a loose football jersey; though it had been over a decade since he'd seen him, Brendan knew without a doubt that it was Whale.

Brendan wheeled around and shot toward the back exit, pulling out his cell phone and punching in Li's number. He'd tell her to grab her things—passport, money, jewelry.

Only what was necessary and what she could carry. He'd tell her to get his leather toiletry kit, too, and then he'd say to meet him at the park near their apartment. If she asked any questions, he'd say that he'd explain everything later, when there was time. They'd head to a bank and take out as much cash as they could, then get a taxi to the airport and get on the next flight to Hong Kong, and then from there, maybe on to Laos or Cambodia. But before he could say anything, the call went straight to her voicemail.

He hung up without leaving a message. Then he went out through the back door. His heart shook his entire body, echoing the frenetic drumming that he had been listening to just moments before.

He sprinted up the alley as soon as he stepped outside, huffing through his gaping mouth. Then he stopped, feeling as if his bladder would give. Sean stood waiting for him there, smoking a cigarette and blocking his path as if he were out on a Sunday stroll. Aside from a few streaks of gray in his hair and some deeper lines around his eyes, Sean looked exactly as he had the last time Brendan had seen him.

"Long time no see," Sean said, and his grin was murderous.

CHAPTER NINE

S EAN scanned the area behind the bakery.

"So this is where you been hiding all these years?" he said.

Brendan said nothing.

"You really surprised me," said Sean. "I didn't think you had it in you."

"Do I know you?"

"Spare me the act, Brendan. We know it's you."

Brendan looked toward Whale, who stood at the end of the alley leading to the street. Then he glanced sideways toward the chain-link fence at the other end of the alley.

"Don't even think about it," said Sean. "Ducie and J.J. are outside your place as we speak. You run, and they'll put the hurt on that wife and kid of yours."

Brendan said nothing. He couldn't think of a single thing to say that wouldn't make matters worse.

"I bet you're wondering how we found you?" asked Sean. "I can see the little wheels turning in your head." Before Brendan could reply, Sean continued: "Facial recognition software. Everyone's using it these days: Google, Facebook, fucking Microsoft. They even used it at the Super Bowl to look for terrorists and ended up finding twenty criminals. Look, ma… I ain't going to Disneyworld!"

Sean took another drag as he laughed at his own joke.

"What do you want?" asked Brendan.

"What do you think I want?"

"Fuck if I know."

"Don't pretend."

"Pretend what?"

"A few weeks after you disappeared, we all got nabbed."

"What?"

"They couldn't pin the bodies on us, but Ducie and Whale got nickels on other charges. J.J. and I would've, too, if it weren't for mishandled evidence."

Brendan felt like throwing up; he'd never once considered what might happen after he'd left New York City. All he'd thought about was getting away and starting over.

"I had nothing to do with that," he said.

"Bullshit."

"I didn't."

"Prove it."

Brendan said nothing.

"You can't, can you?" said Sean. "Right after you disappear, we all get nailed, and here you are hiding out on the other side of the world under a fake name. Even if you didn't rat, that shit ain't right and you know it."

"So you're here to kill me?" asked Brendan.

"If we were here to kill you, you'd already be dead."

"What do you want?"

"You're gonna make things right," said Sean. "This country's practically printing money, and everyone's afraid it's gonna be worthless, so they're all spending it—on apartments, cars, jewelry. The shit's everywhere, and there's hardly any police."

"So?"

"So there's this diamond merchant my cousins know. They move a ton of stuff. Big stuff, too. Four, five-carat stones. And here's the kicker—they hardly have any security at all. Just a few cameras and a fence."

Brendan felt his stomach turn. "No fucking way," he said.

"This isn't a request."

"I'm not doing it."

"You don't do it, Ducie's gonna kill you."

"What does he want me for? I haven't done anything like this in years."

"It's like riding a bike."

Brendan shook his head but said nothing.

"You speak Shanghainese, right?" said Sean. "And you know this city."

"So?"

"So we need someone who does. And we need a can-opener. Someone with experience."

"What about your cousins?"

"Are you kidding? My cousins burn DVDs. They helped us get into China, but they ain't cut out for this shit."

"I'm done with that."

"No, you're not. You can get rid of your ink and call yourself John or Yao Hàn or whatever the fuck you want, but that don't change a thing and you know it."

Brendan said nothing.

"I'm doing you a favor here," said Sean. "You know how Ducie wanted to do this? He wanted to grab your wife and kid and cuff 'em to a radiator till this was done. And that's assuming he was even planning on letting them go once it's over."

Before Brendan could reply, Hamilton came out through the bakery's back door.

"I finished cleaning up, sir," he said. "Is there anything else you need?"

"No," said Brendan. "You can go now."

"Hang on there, sport," said Sean.

He turned to Brendan.

"You guys make Chinese crullers?"

"What?"

"You know," said Sean. "*You char kway* or whatever the fuck they're called. My *nai nai* used to make them for me when I was a kid."

Brendan turned back to Hamilton. "Can you get him some *youtiao*?" he asked.

"Yes, sir."

Sean shook his head as Hamilton went back into the bakery. "You're really playing this shit up, aren't you?" he said. "You're a better actor than I thought."

Brendan said nothing. Sean took one last drag off his cigarette before flicking the butt to the street. After a moment, Hamilton returned with a paper bag filled with *youtiao* and gave them to Sean.

"Thanks, bro," said Sean.

After Hamilton went back inside, Sean turned back to

Brendan. "You got one hour," he said. "Go tell your wife you're gonna be late tonight and start clearing your schedule. Then meet us over at Bar Rouge. You know the place I'm talking about?"

Brendan nodded; it was a huge club downtown overlooking the Bund.

"How will I find you?" he asked.

"Don't worry," said Sean. "We'll find you. And don't get any stupid ideas, like going to the authorities or trying to run. You're a fugitive, too. We'll be watching you. You try anything, and you'll regret it."

Without waiting for a reply, Sean turned and started up the alley. He pulled one of the long, crusty *youtiao* from the bag and bit into it as he walked off.

"Damn," he said. "These ain't half bad."

CHAPTER TEN

BRENDAN stopped at a market on his way back to the apartment and bought some cigarettes. He needed something to help him think, something to steady his nerves. He got one of the local brands—Double Happiness. The package had a bright red ligature on it with a twinned set of the Chinese character for joy. It almost looked like a man gazing into a mirror, Brendan thought as he paid for them. He had the cellophane wrapper off before he even stepped outside and quickly lit one up.

The initial drag went down like a sock full of broken glass. It was the first cigarette he had in over a decade, and he fought the urge to cough as he exhaled. The second drag went down easier, like cheap vodka. His shoulders began to loosen, and he felt the nicotine entering his bloodstream. The third drag went down painlessly, like the hot, dry air from his oven, and he was smoking again as if he'd never quit.

He considered his options while walking home. He could try to run, but what good would that do? Li and Xiaodan would be dead, and there was no way he'd be able to live with that. He could call the authorities, but he was a fugitive himself. As Sean pointed out, turning them in would be turning himself in as well. He could always go get

Li and Xiaodan and try to bolt. Maybe he could create a
diversion, start a fire at their apartment building or call the
police or something. Or maybe they could sneak off down
one of the back alleys or out through the basement. But
even if they got away from Ducie and the others, what then?
Everything he had was tied up in the bakery, and for all he
knew, he'd get stopped at the border or at an airport with
the stolen passport. And if Ducie and the others turned him
in, it would be even harder to move around. Sure, he was a
tabula rasa, but he'd be a wanted white man in a country full
of Chinese people. Being a blank slate only went so far, and
that was assuming Li would even be willing to leave with
him in the first place.

He glanced at his watch as he approached his block.
Only ten minutes had passed since Sean had left him at the
bakery. He still had plenty of time to get down to the Bund,
and he wanted to think some more, to see if there were any
other options he hadn't thought of. So he stopped off at the
park on the corner of Hunan and Xingguo.

He found an empty bench and sat down, then finished
his cigarette and lit another. He tried to think of any alternatives he had other than going to meet them. Perhaps there
was something he was overlooking, some option he might
not have considered, but the harder he thought about it, the
bleaker the situation seemed, and the clearer it became that
there were no trap doors or other ways out.

Then the thought occurred to him that there was
another alternative, a darker and more fatalistic one. But in
order to carry that one out, he would need a gun. And even

if he managed to get one in a country that didn't allow them, he'd then have to walk into a crowded bar full of witnesses and kill four people, most of whom were killers themselves. Even if he had it in him to pull it off, which he wasn't sure of, the chances of getting away with it were far from good.

He mulled it over as he took one last drag off the cigarette. Then he stubbed the cigarette out underneath his shoe. He leaned back against the bench and closed his eyes, and he listened to the sounds all around him: ballroom music playing on a portable CD player, the chattering of the pensioners' caged thrushes and mynah birds, someone practicing the clapping and foot-slapping exercises of *qigong*. He could hear conversations in Shanghainese, barking dogs, car horns, and the rest of the soundtrack of the city.

He thought about praying. But what would he pray for? he wondered. The strength to carry out a crime? Or the strength to commit murder? Did God or whatever was out there listen to prayers that asked for what he was thinking about doing? He wasn't so sure. He knew there was no point in praying for things to disappear; that much was certain. Things didn't just go away like that—at least they never had done so for him.

He eventually just stopped thinking about it at all. He stopped thinking about prayer, and he stopped thinking about alternatives, and he stopped thinking, period. He knew there was only one way out of it that he could see—no amount of thought or prayer would change that.

"You're not actually thinking about going through with this, are you?"

Brendan opened his eyes and saw Tommy sitting on the bench next to him. The blood dripping from his mask was still as wet as if he'd just been shot.

"You know this won't end up good," said Tommy.

Brendan said nothing.

"Haven't you learned anything these past few years?"

"It's just one job," said Brendan.

"That's what everyone says," said Tommy. "Just one job, just one time, just one fix. But you and I both know there ain't no such thing."

Brendan didn't reply.

"You know I'm right," said Tommy.

Brendan closed his eyes and took a deep breath. He listened to the chattering birds for a while. Then he opened his eyes again. Tommy was gone, but everything else was still there. The old men were there, with their caged mynahs and thrushes. The ballroom dancers were there, gliding across the center of the park. The *mahjong* players were there, sitting at the tables and slapping down their tiles—and surely Ducie and the others were still there somewhere, waiting for him.

After another moment, Brendan stood up and walked home.

Li and Xiaodan sat at the kitchen table. Xiaodan rocked back and forth in her high chair and waved her plastic spork in the air as Li cut her food.

"I do!" said Xiaodan. "I do!"

"Yeah, I know," said Li. "You do everything yourself, right?"

Brendan opened the door and entered the apartment.

"*Bàba!*" shouted Xiaodan.

He forced a smile as he walked over to the kitchen and got a glass from the cupboard.

"How'd it go today?" asked Li.

"Fine," he said, filling the glass with water from the dispenser.

"Business good?"

"Mmm-hmm."

He drank the water and refilled the glass. Xiaodan shoveled a giant forkful of broccoli into her mouth.

"Trees!" she said.

Brendan walked over and kissed Xiaodan on the head.

"How about one for me?" asked Li.

He looked up at her, his thoughts clearly elsewhere. She puckered up, and he leaned in and kissed her.

"Ugh," she said. "You taste like an ashtray."

Before Brendan could reply, Xiaodan threw up her arms and shouted.

"All done!" she said.

"Go play with your toys," said Li.

She lifted Xiaodan from the high chair and took off her bib. Then she set her down on the floor and turned her attention back to Brendan as Xiaodan ran tottering into the living room.

"So did you get my message?" she asked.

"What message?"

"I told Hamilton to remind you to get mangoes."

"Shit," he said, suddenly remembering. It felt as if a lifetime had passed since their walk through the park.

"Don't worry about it," she said. "I'll get them on my way back."

"Way back from what?"

"I'm meeting Sophie tonight, remember?"

"But there's something I gotta take care of."

"John—"

He interrupted her. "Sorry, but it can't wait."

"Is it those guys who came to the bakery?"

He perked up. "What guys?"

"Hamilton told me some guys came to see you," she said. "He said you got into an argument with one of them?"

His stomach roiled; he wondered how much Hamilton had heard.

"Is everything all right?" she asked.

"We were just talking."

"Who are they?"

"Just some old friends."

"From America?"

He nodded.

"What are they doing here?" she asked.

"Just passing through."

"Why don't you have them over?"

"Some other time."

"Is something wrong?"

"No."

"John—"

He cut her off again, his voice raised. "Nothing's wrong, all right?"

His angry response startled her. He took a deep breath and waited for a moment before continuing in a calmer voice.

"I'm sorry," he said. "I didn't mean to raise my voice. It's just been a crazy day, that's all."

She said nothing, clearly rattled by his outburst.

"As soon as I take care of a few things, it'll all be over," he continued. "You can go out tomorrow night, okay? You can go every night next week if you want. I promise."

She forced a smile. It surprised him how easy it was to lie to her. It almost felt too easy somehow, and it made him feel bad; it made him think of the character from the Kurosawa film.

"Elmo!"

Brendan and Li turned to see Xiaodan running toward them with a book in her hands. The book was so big compared to her that she looked like a surfer carrying a long board.

"Elmo!" she said, jabbing the book into Brendan's shins. "Elmo!"

He knelt down next to her.

"I can't tonight," he said.

"How about some teddy crackers?" asked Li.

Xiaodan dropped the book and followed Li into the kitchen. Brendan watched them for a moment before turning and walking back toward the bedroom.

He went into the closet and turned on the light. Then he glanced over his shoulder to make sure Li and Xiaodan were still in the kitchen. After he was certain they were, he got a chair from the other room and brought it into the closet. Then he stood on it and moved aside one of the ceiling panels. A moment later, he pulled out his leather toiletry kit.

He opened the toiletry kit and took out his stolen passport and a few banded stacks of hundred-yuan notes. Then he took out a balisong. He popped the latch on the bottom of the balisong's safe handle and clumsily flipped it open. Its partially serrated stainless-steel blade glinted in the light. He'd purchased the knife years before from one of the back-alley sellers at the Dongtai Lu antique market, hoping he'd never need it. And so far, he hadn't. In fact, he had almost forgotten he still had it.

He touched the blade's edge with his finger; even though it had been years since he'd opened the knife, the blade was still as sharp as a razor. He flipped the knife closed and then open again, closed and then open. He used to be able to fan the knife open and closed with ease, but it had been ages since he'd held it. He flipped it open and closed a few more times until he got quicker at it; he still wasn't as fast or as graceful as he'd been before, but for now, it would have to do.

Brendan closed the knife and slipped it into his pocket. He hesitated for a moment before turning off the light and heading toward the door.

CHAPTER ELEVEN

BRENDAN hailed a taxi at an intersection near his apartment building and told the driver to take him to the Bund. The driver cleared his throat and spat out the window, then pulled away from the curb and merged into traffic.

Brendan gazed out at the layered city as it scrolled by. There were so many different Shanghais, next to and on top of one another. There was the Shanghai of the past in the labyrinthine alleyways, *shíkùmén* architecture, and colonial relics of the bygone concession era, and there was the Shanghai of the present and future in the towering construction cranes, bustling markets, and ever-expanding skyline of Pudong. There were rich Westerners and locals in gleaming new Maseratis and Bentleys, and there were poor migrants pulling wooden carts and piled three or four or even five onto a single battery-powered moped. There were gated communities and luxury penthouse apartments rising high in the sky, and there were *cheng zhong cun* made up of old shipping containers and corrugated-metal shacks that had no plumbing or electricity. Yet as disparate as it all seemed, it all came together somehow into one unified and dynamic system, inseparable and complementary parts of a whole, like the *yin yang*.

It reminded Brendan of New York City, and of New York City's many faces: uptown and downtown, the high-rises and the projects, the East Side and the West Side, and the poor and the rich. And the more he thought about it, the more he thought about himself and about his own past and present: Rikers inmate and small businessman, thief and baker, user and abstainer, loner and family man. New York City native and Shanghailander expatriate. Brendan Lavin and John Davis. When the time came, he wondered, could he be the old Brendan again? And if so, would he be able to step out of that role as simply as he stepped back into it when everything was over, as if it were just a familiar article of clothing? Would he be able to return to the new cautious and temperate John? Would he be able to keep the two selves separate, or would they collide and tear each other apart? And were they even separate at all, or were they both always there, like the halves of the *yin yang*, impossible to consider without one another?

By the time they reached the row of historic old stone and brick buildings lining the western side of the Huangpu River, Brendan was no closer to coming up with any answers to his questions. If anything, he'd only come up with even more questions. But it didn't matter—all that mattered was that he had a job to do, and if he wanted to keep the life he had, he needed to do it. In a few days, one way or another, it would all be over, and everything that needed to be answered would be answered somehow. That much was clear.

After he paid the driver and got out, Brendan glanced across the river at the carnivalesque skyline of Pudong. The brand new buildings towered toward the heavens. It looked like something out of a science-fiction movie—*Blade Runner*, maybe, or *Metropolis*. It was the *yang* to the *yin* of the Bund, whose majestic old skyline looked like something from a late nineteenth-century lithograph.

He walked through Huangpu Park, the small triangular expanse of green at the northern end of the Bund. He glanced at his watch as he passed the large bronze statue of Chen Yi, the first communist mayor of Shanghai. It had been fifty-five minutes since Sean had left him at the bakery. The sun had gone down, and the kaleidoscope of lights across the river illuminated the darkening sky.

Brendan crossed the park and walked toward Zhongshan Lu. Tourists mobbed the area, which was why he usually avoided it. They clutched bags of overpriced souvenirs from Nanjing Lu and drank Starbucks coffee and *bobà naichá* from the Taiwanese teashops, and they stood in clusters taking pictures of both skylines with their cameras and smartphones.

He waited at the crosswalk for the light to change. After it finally did, a few cars and mopeds continued to go through the intersection. It was China, after all, and pedestrians never had the right of way.

Brendan crossed as soon as there was an opening, then went into the lobby of Number 18 on the Bund. He found a bank of elevators and took one of them to the top floor, where a wall of cigarette smoke, expensive cologne, and hair products hit him as soon as the elevator doors opened. Clusters of businessmen in Armani and Hugo Boss suits mingled with Eurotrash and gold-digging locals while well-dressed French bartenders served up expensive drinks. Chunky house music thumped loudly in the background.

Brendan walked past the bouncer at the entry and made his way across the bar. Inside, there were more Westerners in expensive suits, skinny Europeans with too-tight clothing, and heavily made-up local girls. There were Chinese businessman, rich American college students, and well-dressed *tai tais*. But for all the people who were there, Sean and the others were nowhere to be seen.

Brendan checked his watch again when he reached the far end of the bar, where an outdoor patio looked out onto the Huangpu and the Pudong skyline behind it. It was now an hour and ten minutes after Sean had left him at the bakery. He began to get nervous. Sean had said to meet him at Bar Rouge, hadn't he? Or had he said Barbarossa? Or had he said Bar Rouge, but meant Barbarossa? He couldn't remember.

He turned around and headed back toward the other end of the bar. Could they be thinking he was trying to run? he wondered. His pulse quickened. Then another thought occurred to him: what if they had just been trying to get him away from Li and Xiaodan so they could take them while he was out? Could that be what this was all about? Revenge?

His stomach roiled. He picked up his pace and continued to scan the crowd, but Sean was nowhere in sight. He glanced at his watch again when he got back to the point he had started from. It was now an hour and twenty minutes after Sean had left him at the bakery.

Brendan's fear became full-blown panic. He went out onto the patio again. Then he looked down at the queue of taxis lined at the curb of Zhongshan Lu. He considered going down there and taking one back to his apartment, but at that time of day and on a Friday night, he figured it would easily take a half hour with the traffic, if not more. And what if they were only running late? What if leaving now would only precipitate some tragic outcome?

He looked around the bar one last time and scanned the faces in the crowd. None of them looked familiar. He recalled something else from P.S. 70, a line of poetry in his ninth-grade English class. *Petals on a wet, black bough.* Then he looked over the faces again—still he saw no one he recognized.

Just as he was about to give up and call Li, he noticed the back of someone who looked like Sean ducking into one of the private rooms. Brendan made his way across the crowded floor and opened the door. Before he could react, two beefy hands yanked him inside and threw him to the floor; a voice spoke from a darkened corner of the room.

"Get the door."

Brendan glanced around as someone closed the door behind him. Whale knelt right next to him, holding him down. J.J. was standing by the door. In the intervening years, he'd swapped one bad look for another, trading his chinstrap beard and frosted tips for earplugs and a fauxhawk. Sean sat at a table covered with bottles of Grey Goose and Cristal, and Ducie lurked in a corner. A thick scar ran diagonally across the right side of Ducie's face, something he'd picked up since the last time Brendan had seen him. It cut through his right eye, which was now covered over with a milky gray cataract; his other eye gleamed in the dim light, and he held a pistol in one hand.

Whale found the balisong in Brendan's pocket and tossed it to Ducie. Ducie fanned it open and shook his head.

"Naughty little doggie," he said.

"Wait—"

Before Brendan could finish, Ducie turned to Sean. "Get me a cushion," he said.

"What?"

"You didn't actually think I was gonna let you live, did you?"

Sean yanked a pillow off a nearby couch and tossed it to Ducie.

"I came willingly," said Brendan.

"So what?" said Ducie. "You're a fucking rat."

"No, I'm not—"

Ducie moved forward and put the pillow against Brendan's head. Brendan squirmed in Whale's grip as Ducie pointed the pistol against the pillow.

"It wasn't me—"

"Then why did you run?"

"What?"

"Why the fuck did you run?"

"'Cause I wanted to start over."

"Bullshit."

"I swear to God, I'm telling the truth."

"Say goodbye, asshole."

Ducie turned his face as if to prepare for the blowback. "No!"

He pulled the trigger: a plastic firing pin clicked against an empty cylinder.

"What the hell?"

Ducie laughed. "Got you," he said. "It's a toy. See?"

He pulled the trigger a few more times. The plastic firing pin of the toy gun clicked again and again.

"Are you crazy?" said Brendan.

Ducie turned to the others. "He thought I was gonna kill him," he said, laughing.

"What the hell's the matter with you?"

"I wanted to hear what you had to say."

"I didn't rat."

"I don't give a fuck if you did or not," said Ducie. "What's done is done, and now you're gonna do something for us, or I will end you for real. Are we understood?"

Brendan said nothing. Whale shoved him in the back.

"Answer him," he said.

Brendan nodded.

"Good," said Ducie.

He reached out and grabbed Brendan by the chin. "Brendan fucking Lavin," he said, slapping Brendan's face. "It's good to see you."

Brendan shoved him away. "Fuck off," he said.

Ducie turned to the others and grinned. "You see that?" he said. "He's still got his stones."

CHAPTER TWELVE

J.J. finished off the last of the Grey Goose.

"Where the hell's the waitress?" he said.

"Welcome to China," said Sean. "The service here's terrible."

Ducie pulled out a wad of hundred-yuan notes and gave some to J.J.

"Go get us another bottle, will you?" he said.

"Some burgers, too," said Whale.

J.J. left the room. Ducie turned to Brendan.

"So," he said, "aren't you even curious?"

"About what?" said Brendan.

"About the fucking job, what do you think?"

Brendan didn't reply.

"It was Sean's idea," said Ducie. "I would've just put a bullet in your head and dumped you in a ditch. Hell, I still might if you even so much as think about trying anything."

"Do you even know what you're getting yourself into?" asked Brendan. "This isn't America here."

"No shit."

"These cops don't mess around. The last guy that robbed a bank got hunted down like an animal. They shot him eight times—no Miranda rights, no trial. Nothing. He wasn't even armed."

"So?"

"So do you even have guns?"

"Not yet, but we're getting them."

"How?"

"Sean's taking care of it."

"They're illegal."

"So what?"

"No, I mean *illegal* illegal. Zero-tolerance illegal. You get life here for committing a crime with a gun, and that's if they don't kill you first—not to mention the fact they're impossible to get."

"Nothing's impossible here," said Sean. "You can buy sex. Drugs. Hell, you can buy a fucking kidney if you want. A bunch of guys sold theirs to buy iPads and shit. I saw it on CNN."

"Relax, will you?" said Ducie. "The only thing you need to worry about is popping a can, so have a drink or something and just lighten the fuck up."

Before Brendan could reply, J.J. returned with another bottle of Grey Goose. The bruising baseline of the house music washed over the room for a moment until the door swished closed again.

The PICK U LIKE MOVY store stood between a hair salon and a Uyghur restaurant. Two expats came out with a plastic bag full of bootleg DVDs; at the corner of the street, a street vendor roasted chestnuts in a blackened wok.

Brendan and the others approached the store. Sean stopped at the door.

"Wait here," he said.

He went inside. Brendan took out his cigarettes and shook one out. He counted how many were left as he lit it: there were twelve, which meant he'd already smoked eight since buying the pack. Maybe he should start pacing himself, he thought.

J.J. looked at the display window full of movie posters and shook his head.

"Unbelievable," he said. "They just sell this shit right out in the open. They don't give a fuck about copyright or nothing?"

No one replied.

"I gotta give it to the Chinese," said J.J. "They got some set of balls."

"It ain't balls they got," said Ducie. "They just don't have anything worth ripping off yet. But wait until they do. We'll see how much of a fuck they give about copyright when they got some skin in the game."

J.J. turned to Brendan and gestured to the DVDs. "You watch these?" he asked.

Brendan nodded.

"The quality's good?"

"Most of the time," said Brendan.

"Nothing's ever as good as the real thing," said Ducie. "I got a fake Rolex once, made by some watchmaker in Korea. He even used 18-karat gold for it, just like the real ones have. I'd show it to people and they couldn't tell, but I knew."

He looked at Brendan before continuing.

"You can always spot a fake if you're looking closely," he said.

Brendan turned away and took a long drag off the cigarette. A moment later, Sean exited the store, followed by a wiry thirty-year-old in skinny black jeans and a bright orange Jägermeister t-shirt.

"Hey, everybody," said Sean. "This is my cousin, Bodhi."

Bodhi clumsily flashed a three-fingered gang sign.

"Wassup, guys?" he said.

They took Line 5 of the Shanghai Metro out to the Minhang District; Bodhi pointed things out to them along the way. He'd learned most of his English from movies like *Road House* and *Point Break*, the latter being the source of his English name.

After they got off at the final stop, Bodhi led them from the station to the empty streets of the Minhang Development Zone, home to many of Shanghai's factories and production facilities. Most of the workers had already gone home for the day, back to their cramped hovels and *cheng zhong cun;* at night, the area was a ghost town.

They followed Bodhi down an alleyway and through a hole in a chain-link fence. He led them to a darkened factory that appeared abandoned. Brendan stopped when they approached a rusty metal roll-up door.

"I don't know about this," he said.

"Trust me, brah," said Bodhi. "It's cool."

Bodhi rolled up the door, and they followed him inside.

He led them to a large floor full of broken-down die-press machines and turned on some lights. Warped and cut-up mesh sheets used to make sneaker liners littered the floor.

"So where are these guys?" asked Brendan.

"Chill out," said Bodhi. "They'll be here."

"When?"

"Soon, brah. Soon."

Whale kicked an empty beer bottle across the floor. After a moment, a door clanged open in another part of the factory; another moment later, three young Fujianese men with shaved heads and baggy black clothing entered from a stairwell. Bodhi said something in Mandarin that Brendan didn't catch, and the men responded in a guttural, flat-tongued Fuzhou dialect that made it sound as if they were coughing up their words. It was even harder for Brendan to understand than Cantonese, but it was clear that they were angry.

"What'd they say?" asked J.J.

"Something about finding the place," said Sean.

"No, they didn't," said Brendan. "They're pissed off. Your cousin was only supposed to bring one of us here."

Ducie spoke before Sean could reply. "Where are the guns?" he said.

Bodhi spoke to the Fujianese men again, and one of them responded.

"He wants to know where the money is," said Bodhi.

"Fuck that," said Ducie. "Show us the guns first."

This time, Brendan almost understood Bodhi's Mandarin translation, but he could not follow the reply.

"He says no money, no guns," said Bodhi.

"This is bullshit," said J.J.

"Just show him the money," said Bodhi.

Ducie pulled out a two-inch-thick stack of hundred-yuan notes.

"See?" he said. "We got money. Now where are the motherfucking guns?"

After Bodhi translated, the men conversed among themselves for a moment before one of them pulled out a smartphone and sent a text message.

"What the fuck is going on?" said Whale.

"Just be cool, cuz," said Bodhi.

After a moment, the door clanged open again in the other part of the factory. Another moment later, a burly young Fujianese entered from the stairwell, carrying a large black duffel bag. He brought it over to the other Fujianese men, and the leader of the group unzipped it and stepped forward to show them its contents. Inside the bag were a dozen new-looking pistols with the serial numbers filed off. Most of them were Chinese-made Norinco QSZ-92 services pistols, the official handgun of the People's Liberation Army. There were a few NP-22s and NZ-75s as well, Norinco knockoffs of German Sig-Sauer P226s and Czech CZ 75s.

"Now we're talking," said Sean.

"How much?" asked Ducie.

Bodhi translated, and the leader responded.

"Ten thousand," said Bodhi.

"For all of them?" asked Ducie.

"No," said Bodhi. "Ten thousand each."

"Is he fucking crazy?" said Ducie.

"That's how they do it here," said Brendan. "Everything starts out high. Tell him you'll give him five."

"I'll give him two."

"Things cost more here—"

"The fuck they do."

He turned to Bodhi and held up two fingers. "Tell him two thousand each," he said.

This time, no translation was necessary: the Fujianese men understood the gesture and their leader answered before Bodhi could speak.

"He says nine," said Bodhi.

"No fucking way," said Ducie. "Tell him three and that's as high as I go."

Bodhi said this in Mandarin to the Fujianese men; the leader laughed and shook his head.

"What the fuck's his problem?" said Ducie.

The leader nodded to Ducie and said something to his men, and they all laughed.

"Fuck this motherfucking chink—"

The leader took offense to what Ducie said and cursed at him.

"What's the matter?" said Ducie. "You don't like being called a chink, you yellow piece of shit?"

They stepped forward and got in each other's faces, both shouting in languages unintelligible to the other aside from obvious swears and slurs. The other Fujianese men stepped forward to back up their leader and J.J., Whale, and Sean did the same, but Brendan and Bodhi stepped in between before any punches were thrown.

"Enough," said Brendan.

"Fuck this guy," said Ducie.

Bodhi spoke to the others in Mandarin again. Everyone stood his ground, waiting for the next move from Ducie or the leader.

After a moment, Ducie turned to Bodhi.

"Tell him I'll give him four each," he said. "Final offer."

Bodhi hesitated.

"Tell him," said Ducie.

Bodhi translated, and the leader mulled it over.

"Fuck this shit," said Ducie. "We're done here."

Ducie turned to leave; Whale and the others followed. Before they got far, the leader of the Fujianese men said something. Ducie and the others stopped and looked back.

"What'd he say?" asked Ducie.

"He says he'll give them to you for five," said Bodhi.

Ducie hesitated for a moment before speaking. "Done," he said.

He took out his stack of money and began paying the leader. J.J. and Sean selected pistols from the bag. The burly young Fujianese man approached Whale and gestured to Bodhi with a smartphone.

"What the fuck does he want?" asked Whale.

"He wants a picture with the African," said Bodhi.

"I ain't no motherfucking African."

"Just let him get a picture," said Sean.

"This is bullshit."

The burly young Fujianese man reached up and put his arm around Whale, grinning. Whale forced a smile through gritted teeth.

"Fuck this motherfucker," he said.

Bodhi snapped a picture. Brendan took out his pack of cigarettes with a trembling hand and opened it; there were only ten left. *Better pace myself*, he thought, closing the pack. Then he opened it again and shook one out.

Fuck it, he thought. He'd quit again when this was all over.

They walked back to the subway station and got on a northbound 5 train. J.J. carried a knapsack containing two QSZ-92 services pistols and two NP-22s. After a few stops, they got off and switched to Line 1. The car they'd gotten on was packed, so they stood in the center.

Brendan looked at the sea of people around them as they rode back toward the center of Shanghai—they were all Chinese, and many of them were staring. One little girl was mesmerized by Ducie and stood gazing at the scar on his face from behind her father's legs. After a moment, Ducie lunged at her with his hands up and made a face.

"Boo!" he said.

For a moment, it looked like the girl was going to cry. Then she burst out laughing. Ducie stuck out his tongue and rolled his eyes and made another funny face, and the girl laughed even harder. Even Whale couldn't help but smile.

They rode through two more stops and got off at

Hengshan Lu. At the station's exit, they passed a migrant woman grilling skewers of various meats and vegetables over a bed of hot coals. Ducie bought a skewer of grilled scorpions from her and bit into one of them as they walked away.

"Damn," he said. "These are killer." He offered the skewer to Brendan. "Want one?"

Brendan shook his head.

"Suit yourself," said Ducie.

He bit another scorpion off the skewer and swallowed it whole, grinning. Brendan turned away and lit another cigarette.

They continued on, making their way to Gao'an Lu. They passed a massage parlor and a sex shop selling colorful dildos and bondage gear. Then they passed a tattoo parlor where the walls were covered with *irezumi* and Ed Hardy-style flashing. At Huaihai Lu, they headed west until they reached the old art deco-style Normandie Apartments. Then they turned north onto Wukang. Ducie stopped as they approached the corner of Wukang and Tai'an.

"There it is," he said.

Brendan looked up the block, where a whitewashed, two-story stucco building stood inside a lot surrounded by a high wall crowned with rotating, anti-scale spike fencing. A closed metal gate wide enough for a car to fit through filled the center of the wall; next to the gate was a thick metal door made of the same burnished material. Brendan must have passed the lot a thousand times before without noticing it. There were hundreds just like it in the former French Concession.

"We've been watching it for a few days," said Ducie. "They're normally open ten to six, but it's New Year's Eve tomorrow, so they're only open a half day, and they're probably not expecting much business. Four people are usually there. Two of them are salespeople. One's a Jet Li-looking cat in his thirties; the other looks like that skinny chick from *Kill Bill*. Lulu Who or whatever the fuck it is. There's also an older guy who comes by every day to open, but he always splits before noon. He looks like a fruit and dresses like Willy Wonka. Drives a brand-new orange Lamborghini. He must be the owner. The other one's security. Big guy— always the first to arrive and always the last to go."

"So what's the plan?" asked Brendan.

"We'll steal two minivans in the morning. The city's full of them, so they blend in. The big guy always arrives at ten; the fruit usually shows up just after him. It's a one-way street, so we know which direction they'll be coming from. Whale will be waiting in the getaway vehicle in a nearby alley while Sean's waiting in the other van a block to the south. You, J.J., and I will be on the ground near the intersection. When the Lamborghini passes, I'll contact Sean—he'll block off the traffic back at the intersection. As soon as the big guy opens the gate for the Lamborghini, we'll move. There are at least four security cameras on the lot and another three that I spotted on the block, so we'll all be wearing masks. I'll take out the big guy, and J.J. will grab the fruit. Sean will join us and cover the gate while we go inside and clean out the place. They have two safes—hopefully the fruit will play nice and just open them for us, but if he doesn't, you're on. Only one of them is X6. You should be able to get into the other one easy. If not, we've got a grinder with a tungsten-carbide bit and a portable plasma cutter as well."

"I've never used a plasma cutter," said Brendan.

"You'll do fine," said Sean. "They work just the same as oxy torches."

"The nearest police station is four blocks away," said Ducie. "With that intersection blocked off, we'll have a five-minute window, tops, which means we'll need to be out of there in four. Once we get the stones, Whale will drive us south to Ningbo. Sean's cousin hooked us up with the captain of a cargo ship who'll take us to Malaysia. Ningbo's one of the biggest ports in the world, and everybody's gonna be celebrating New Year's anyway, so we'll slip away no problem. Any questions?"

"What if something goes wrong?"

Ducie glared at Brendan. "Nothing's gonna go wrong," he said.

"But what if something does?"

"There's a whole maze of alleys behind the buildings on this block," said Ducie. "If anything happens to the getaway car or if we get separated, there are at least a half a dozen ways out of here on foot. I have a map of it for you and you can memorize it. You probably already know it, anyway. And I got each of us a burner so we can get in touch with each other if we get separated, but if things actually get that bad, we'll all be better off getting to Ningbo on our own. Any other questions?"

No one replied.

"Good," said Ducie. "Let's get some pussy."

The lobby at Chateau Bacchus KTV looked like something out of a third-rate Las Vegas nightclub, with garish purple interiors and cheap mood lighting. Six hostesses in shimmering dresses bowed and greeted Chinese and Western businessmen as they entered the building. Behind them, bottles of Johnnie Walker Black, Rémy Martin VSOP, and Maotai lined the long shelves of the bar.

After greeting Brendan and the others, one of the hostesses led them to a private room in back. The walls of the private room were lined with couches facing two large flatscreen televisions. One of the televisions had a karaoke menu screen and was set up for selecting songs and ordering drinks; a Real Madrid soccer game played on the other screen.

A server entered the room after them. "Drinks?"

"Chivas," said Ducie.

"Two," said Whale.

"Maker's Mark," said J.J.

"Grey Goose," said Sean.

The server turned to Brendan. "And for you?" she asked.

"I'm fine."

"Bring him some tequila," said Ducie.

"That's all right."

"Bring it anyway in case he changes his mind."

After the server left, Brendan spoke. "I'm gonna go home," he said.

"No, you're not," said Ducie. "You're staying with us until this is done."

"Come on."

"You want to do this the easy way or you want me to have Whale throw you in a fucking closet?"

Brendan said nothing.

"That's what I thought," said Ducie. "Now sit down and have a drink with us. Have a fucking Sprite if you want. I don't give a shit what you do as long as it doesn't interfere with me."

Before Brendan could reply, a petite forty-something *mami* in a conservatively cut pantsuit entered the room. She had harsh, bird-like features and carried a walkie-talkie.

"You want DJ?" she asked.

"For what?" asked Ducie.

"Karaoke."

"Sure, what the hell."

"Girls?"

"Fuck yeah."

The *mami* said something over the walkie-talkie. A moment later, a dozen *zuotai xiaojie* entered the room and lined up by the door, wearing high heels and strapless gold dresses that stopped high above the knee. Each one had a plastic tag clipped to her dress with a three-digit number on it. Most of them were a little rough around the edges and looked like they came from poor country provinces like

Anhui or Gansu rather than Shanghai. Some smiled and giggled while others just looked tired; the oldest one looked like she was in her late twenties, while the youngest couldn't have been more than sixteen.

"You like?" asked the *mami*.

"How do we do this?" asked J.J.

"Just pick girl you want."

"Damn."

Sean pointed to a short curvy girl with a broad face and the number 288 on her tag. "I'll take her," he said.

After the girl went over and sat down next to Sean, the *mami* turned to J.J. next. "For you?" she asked.

J.J. nodded to a girl with the number 517 on her tag. She left the line and approached him. Then the *mami* looked to Whale. He looked over the girls; most of them averted their eyes. He nodded to a tall and voluptuous girl who did not.

"She's good," he said.

Before the *mami* could get to Ducie, he nodded to a skinny girl with short, spiky hair. "I'll take that one," he said. Then he pointed to the girl who looked sixteen. "And that one."

The *mami* turned to Brendan as the two girls approached Ducie. "And you?" she asked.

"None for me," he said.

Ducie pointed to a young girl with the number 401 on her tag. "Leave her, too," he said.

The young girl stepped forward and joined the others. Then the *mami* left the room with the ones they didn't select.

Brendan looked over at Ducie, who was groping both

of the girls he'd chosen. A moment later, the server returned with their drinks.

Brendan stepped into a restroom. The space was dimly lit with a weak red light coming from two shoddily installed wall sconces. Through the thin wall, he could hear a Chinese businessman singing an off-key karaoke rendition of Alphaville's "Forever Young" in one of the other rooms; it sounded like a cat being abused.

Brendan pulled out his cell phone and dialed Li's number. He hoped she wouldn't pick up, but she answered after a few rings, sounding like she'd been sleeping.

"Hello?"

"Hey, baby."

"What's in the background?"

"Nothing."

"It sounds terrible. Where are you?"

"Still out with my friends."

"What time is it?"

"I don't know, but if it ends up being really late, I'll probably just head straight to the bakery."

"John—"

"I'm sorry, babe. The time just got away from me. I'll try and pull away soon if I can, but if I can't, I'll see you tomorrow."

"Don't forget to pick up some *nian gao* for the reunion dinner."

"I won't."

"And make sure it's the kind with rosewater, and not that greasy Shanghainese stuff. My mom hates that."

"All right."

He waited for her to hang up first. Once she did, he began looking for Hamilton's number, but instead of calling him, he wrote Hamilton a text message, telling him to open the bakery by himself. Then he put away his cell phone.

"You're getting really good at this, aren't you?"

Brendan looked up. Tommy was standing next to him in the reflection of the mirror. Blood continued to seep through his torn-up mask.

"Pretty soon you're gonna have a hard time remembering what's a lie and what's the truth," he said.

Brendan said nothing.

"*Oh, what a tangled web we weave, when first we practice to deceive—*"

Brendan closed his eyes and gripped the edges of the sink. He took a deep breath and then slowly let it out. After a long moment, he opened his eyes again and looked into the mirror. Tommy was gone.

On the other side of the wall, the drunken businessman continued to belt out the song.

CHAPTER THIRTEEN

HE dreamed he was a tiger and that he was stalking a gaur calf through a forest. It was early morning, and the fog-shrouded woods were spectral and otherworldly.

He followed the animal's tracks along a windy river for a few miles before they branched off into the forest. From there, he pursued the tracks until they went cold. Then he switched back and crossed the river upstream at a low point. He rediscovered the calf's trail on the other side of the river and followed it into the hills.

The animal's tiny cloven tracks became fractional and obliterated, but he stayed with the trail. He left the spoor and went on ahead when the animal picked up a trodden path, no longer following its movements but instead predicting them. He visualized what the calf was seeing and how it was moving, and when he picked up its tracks again, he was much closer to the animal.

He got down low and pulled himself forward, toward his prey. Before long, he spotted the calf at a watering hole downwind. He moved in to strike, then paused when he heard a branch snap somewhere behind him, but when he turned back, he saw nothing. Alert, he turned and made his way back into the cover of the forest. The second time he heard a branch breaking, he knew with certainty that he was being followed.

He headed deeper into the forest and changed his direction slightly enough so he could make his way up toward a low ridge. He approached an escarpment leading to a plateau and then took cover in a craggy beard of rocks along the side of the hill. Once situated, he turned back to face the tree line; the hair on his back rose as he wondered what it was that might be hunting him. Perhaps it was wolves, or a black bear, or maybe even humans, but before he could find out, he heard a car horn honking nearby. Then he heard another car horn, and then another. He opened his eyes and saw the hotel room and Sean sleeping in the queen-sized bed next to his own.

Brendan looked over toward the window. Outside, it was still dark. He got up from bed and walked over to the bathroom. On his way, he saw Whale through the open partition door, chopping up five thick lines of cocaine on the back of a small mirror in the next room. The knapsack of pistols was on a table, along with some plastic Flexicuffs, latex gloves, a pair of steel slim jims, and a small black sack. J.J. was still asleep on a couch, but Ducie was nowhere to be seen.

Brendan flipped on the bathroom light and closed the door behind him. Then he turned on the faucet and splashed some cold water on his face. He grabbed one of the hotel's towels and dried off, then took out his cell phone and checked his messages. There was a text message from Hamilton in response to the one he'd sent; like every other text Hamilton had sent him, it read, *sure, sir. no problem.* There was also a text from Li. It read, *didn't hear u come in last nite. r u ok? miss you.* :-) He typed in a reply: *i'm fine. went straight to work. miss you too. see you soon.*

Brendan heard the door to the hotel room open outside. He turned off his cell phone and left the bathroom. Ducie was back and was in the other room with Whale; he had a large plastic shopping bag.

"Gather round," he said.

Sean struggled out of bed and pulled on a shirt as he stumbled into the other room. Brendan followed. Ducie pulled several Peking opera masks out of the bag and tossed a red-and-black one to Brendan.

"That one's yours," he said.

He tossed a green mask to Sean and a dark blue one with pointed eyebrows to Whale. Then he gave one to J.J. that had a caricatured white face with flowery pink cheeks.

"What the fuck is this?" asked J.J.

"What?"

"How come I gotta be the clown?"

"Who cares who's the clown?" said Sean.

"If you don't care, then why don't you be the clown?"

"Quit being a fucking baby."

Before J.J. could reply, Ducie opened the knapsack of pistols. He gave the QSZ-92 services pistols to Whale and Sean and one of the NP-22s to J.J. before stuffing the other NP-22 into his own waistband. Then he turned to Brendan.

"You're gonna have to go naked," he said. "But you can have your little pig-sticker back."

Ducie tossed the balisong to Brendan. Whale snorted a fat line of coke off the tray before passing it to Sean. Sean took a line and gave the mirror to J.J., and after J.J. finished, he offered the tray to Brendan, but Brendan shook his head.

"You sure?" asked J.J.

Brendan nodded. Ducie took the tray from J.J. and snorted one of the remaining lines of coke up one nostril, then snorted the final line up his other nostril.

"All right," he said, his eyes widening. "Let's do this."

They left the hotel and went to the maze of streets behind the park in Hongqiao. Drivers left their vehicles there overnight since there were no parking regulations and since it was close to all of the city rings. It was still dark outside, and there was a light rain falling; most of the street lamps had already automatically shut off.

Ducie gave Brendan one of the slim jims when they got to the park.

"Get cracking," he said.

"I'm a little rusty—"

"Better get unrusty, then."

Brendan approached one of the minivans. He chose the oldest-looking one he could find, a silver 2002 Chrysler. Even back when he'd been stealing cars, manufacturers had already been starting to incorporate internal defenses like barrier blocks on the bottoms of the windows or shrouding the operating rods to foil lockout tools. If he was lucky enough, he might be able to find something without either.

He bumped the vehicle first to see if there was an alarm—there wasn't. Then he slipped the hooked end of the slim jim between the van's window and its rubber seal and wiggled it around until it caught the lock mechanism. After he unlocked the door, he got in behind the wheel and cracked open the steering column. None of the wires looked familiar: the traditional yellow, red, and brown wires he was used to were replaced by a corded rainbow of blacks, oranges, light greens, and bright pinks.

He followed the wires as far back as he could and was able to rule out the black one. There were two bright pink wires, and since that was the only color there were two of, he assumed they were the primary power supply and the connection for the vehicle's electrical circuits. But he was unsure whether the orange or the green wire was the ignition.

"Hurry up," said Ducie.

Brendan stripped and twisted together the bright pink wires. He hesitated for a moment before selecting the orange wire, then stripped it and touched its exposed end to the exposed ends of the twisted pink wires. Nothing happened. Ducie shook his head, but before he could say anything, Brendan touched the wires together once more, and the engine sputtered to life.

He got out of the vehicle. J.J. got in behind the wheel and Sean climbed into the passenger's seat. They drove off as Brendan approached another older minivan. He slipped the slim jim in between its window and its rubber seal, then jiggled it around until he managed to unlock the door. He got in and checked the visor and glove compartment for a spare set of keys, but there weren't any, so he proceeded to break the steering column. Then he looked under the steering wheel and found the wires for the ignition switch and the electrical circuits. Unlike the other minivan, the wires were the traditional reds, yellows, and browns. He quickly stripped them and twisted them together, then found the ignition wire and touched it to the others, and the engine coughed to life.

Ducie approached the minivan. Before he could get there, a skinny, bare-chested Chinese man in frayed pajama bottoms came running out through the front door of a nearby hovel. He yanked open the driver's side door of the minivan and yelled and beat at Brendan with his fists. Whale rushed forward and pulled the QSZ-92 from his waistband, then grabbed the Chinese man by the back of the neck. He smashed the man in the temple with the butt of his gun, and the man went slack. He let the man's limp body fall to the pavement.

"Let's go," said Ducie.

Whale opened the driver's side door and got behind the wheel. Ducie rode shotgun; Brendan sat in back.

Brendan glanced over his shoulder at the unconscious man as they drove off, feeling as if he was watching a movie he'd somehow already seen.

They drove back to the center of the Changning district and met the others on a quiet side street by Huashan Park.

By the time they arrived, the weak sun was already up in the pallid, concrete-colored sky, and traffic filled the rain-slicked streets. Out on the sidewalks, locals bought produce at wet markets while expatriates and the wealthy walked their purebred dogs; a trio of old women practiced *tai chi* in a park, moving like synchronized swimmers in slow motion.

On the side street, they switched the license plates of the vans with some license plates Ducie had stolen the day before. Then Sean drove off in one of the vans while Whale left in the other. From there, Brendan, J.J., and Ducie set out on foot. Brendan carried a black duffel bag containing the portable plasma cutter and the grinder; together, they weighed about fifty pounds. He switched the bag from one shoulder to the other at the end of every block.

At ten minutes to ten, as the rain began to let up, they pulled up their hoods and put on their sunglasses, even though there was no sun in the sky. Brendan felt his heartbeat begin to accelerate. He felt the way he used to feel before a fight was about to happen, or before going all in during a game of Texas Hold 'Em.

At five minutes to ten, they reached the block where the diamond merchant's building stood; they could tell no one had arrived yet when they were close enough to see it, so they slowly continued walking north. A few minutes later, a large man in a plain black suit approached the building on foot and unlocked the door next to the gate. Brendan recognized him as the one Ducie described as the security; he wore wraparound Ray-Ban sunglasses and his hair was shorn to the skin. Brendan watched as the man locked the door behind himself after entering the courtyard. Then he followed J.J. and Ducie toward a newsstand near the end of the block.

They looked over the newsstand's magazines while keeping an eye on the gate. 10:05 came and went and nothing happened. So did 10:10, and then 10:15. Someone lit a string of firecrackers in a nearby alley, startling Brendan. A few minutes later, a homeless man on crutches approached them with a dirty hat in his hand and asked them for change. They tried to ignore him for as long as they could, but he persisted until Brendan finally gave him a ten-*kuài* note just to get rid of him.

At 10:20, Brendan turned to Ducie.

"What should we do?" he asked.

Ducie replied without making eye contact. "Nothing," he said. "Just keep waiting."

They crossed the street and began making their way back down the block. At 10:25, Ducie's cell phone rang, and he answered it.

"Yeah?"

Brendan could hear Sean's voice at the other end. "Somebody blocked me in," he said.

"So move them," said Ducie.

J.J. nervously glanced toward the street. "Maybe we should call it off," he said.

"We're not calling it off," said Ducie.

Brendan looked down the street and saw a green and white bus coming in their direction. After it passed, he saw a brand-new Lamborghini Aventador approaching. It came up the street like a Macy's Day Parade float, bright orange and slicked with rain. Even from a distance, he could hear the steady rumble of the car's 6.5-liter V-12 engine. It sounded like an idling fighter plane.

"Look," he said.

Ducie and J.J. looked over and saw the Lamborghini slow as it approached the opening gate. Then Ducie spoke over the cell phone.

"We're on," he said.

He hung up.

"Shouldn't we wait?" asked Brendan.

"For what?" asked Ducie.

Without waiting for a reply, Ducie pulled on a pair of latex gloves. After he had them on, he took out his Peking opera mask and slipped it over his face, and J.J. did the same. Then Ducie drew his NP-22 and held it at his side as he made his way across the street; J.J. followed with his own pistol drawn.

Brendan fumbled out his mask from the waistband of his pants and slipped it on. He pulled on his latex gloves as he hurried across the street after Ducie and J.J., lugging the duffel bag with him. They stormed into the compound behind the Lamborghini as it went through the gate. Once they were inside the compound, Ducie turned to J.J.

"Get the gate," he said.

The large man in the black suit emerged from the building and spoke as J.J. closed the gate.

"*Shénme ta me de?*"

Ducie strode up to the man and pointed the NP-22 in his face.

"On the ground!" he said.

The man hesitated. Ducie smashed him in the nose with the butt of the pistol.

"I said on the ground," said Ducie. "Now."

The man dropped to the ground, blood gushing from his nostrils. Nearby, the man behind the wheel of the Lamborghini revved the engine in reverse, but there was nowhere for him to go—J.J. was closing the gate.

Ducie tossed two pairs of Flexicuffs to Brendan.

"Cuff him," he said.

Brendan put down the duffel bag and cuffed the man's wrists behind his back. Then he cuffed the man's ankles. Ducie approached the driver's-side door of the Lamborghini and tried to open it, but it was locked; inside the car, the owner of the store, a sliver of a man in a purple suit and a cream-colored shirt, fumbled with his cell phone.

"Open up!" shouted Ducie. The owner ignored him, and Ducie shouted again. "Open the fuck up!" he said.

Again, the owner ignored him. Ducie smashed the glass of the driver's side window with the butt of his pistol, then yanked the owner through the window of the car. He took the cell phone from him before shoving him toward the building.

"Move," he said, crushing the owner's cell phone beneath the heel of his boot.

Brendan grabbed the duffel bag and followed Ducie and the owner toward the building. J.J. checked to make sure the gate was locked once he got it closed. Then he shut off the idling engine of the Lamborghini and stood by the door next to the gate.

Once inside, Ducie shoved the owner against the counter.

"Tell this fucker to open the safes," said Ducie.

Brendan translated Ducie's words into Mandarin. The owner shook his head and responded in a panicked voice.

"What's he saying?" asked Ducie.

"He says he can't."

"Bullshit."

"He says they're on a timer—"

Before Brendan could finish, Ducie shot the owner in the knee. The owner dropped the floor, clutching his ruined leg and screaming in pain.

"Jesus…"

Ducie interrupted Brendan. "Get them open," he said. "Now."

Brendan carried the duffel bag behind the counter and looked over the two standing safes. "Which one's not X6?" he said.

"What?"

"You said one of them wasn't X6," said Brendan. "Which one?"

"How the fuck should I know?"

"Are you kidding me?"

"Just open it, will you?"

Brendan looked over the safes. He didn't recognize the make or model of either one—until he saw a tiny Amsec logo on the bottom of the first safe's doors. Amsec was one of the better commercial safe producers in the world, so this one was likely to have six-sided protection. He turned to Ducie and gestured to the other safe.

"Give me a hand," he said.

They struggled to turn the safe around. Brendan took the portable plasma cutter from the duffel bag and looked for an outlet. The owner continued to shriek on the floor and clutch his injured knee, and Ducie kicked him in the stomach.

"Shut the fuck up," he said.

Brendan put on a pair of sunglasses and fired up the plasma cutter. Then he began cutting through the back of the safe. The cutter was a top-of-the-line model with a rated cutting capacity of fifteen inches per minute, far better than any oxy torch Brendan had ever used, but it gave off far more smoke and heat than any oxy torch he'd used as well.

Ducie looked to his watch. "Two minutes," he said.

Outside in the courtyard, J.J. opened the door for Sean and then closed it and locked it again behind him. A moment later, Sean entered the building.

"Well?" he asked. "Where are we?"

"Halfway through," said Brendan.

"Hurry up," said Ducie.

Brendan continued cutting through the safe. Sweat poured down his brow and back. Though it had been over a decade since he'd used a torch, and though he'd never used a plasma cutter before, it all came back to him just like Sean had said it would.

Ducie looked to his watch again. "Thirty seconds," he said.

Brendan continued cutting; the smoke got past his glasses, causing his eyes to water and making it hard for him to see.

"We're out of time," said Ducie.

"Come on," said Sean.

Brendan finished cutting the back of the safe and turned off the plasma cutter. He attached a magnetic handle to the area he'd cut, pulled it off, and let it fall clanking to the floor.

"Got it," he said.

Brendan reached in through the hole in the back of the safe and scooped everything he could into the black sack.

"Let's go," said Ducie.

Before Brendan could finish gathering the contents of the safe, a shot rang out outside.

"What the fuck?" said Sean.

They all turned and watched as a young woman in a pantsuit emerged from a hidden back entrance to the lot, holding a Baby Glock 26. She fired again and hit J.J. in the hip. Before she could fire another shot, Ducie raised his pistol and fired at her, shattering the store's windows, and she returned fire.

"Get down," said Ducie.

Sean ducked outside as Brendan and Ducie hit the floor. The woman fired seven more rapid shots in their direction, shattering windows and display-case panels. Ducie popped back to his feet as soon as she finished firing and returned fire in her direction. Brendan heard Sean and J.J. returning fire outside as well. The woman managed to get off one last shot in their direction and ended up hitting Ducie in the leg.

"Motherfucker," said Ducie.

"You all right?" asked Sean.

Ducie gritted his teeth and trudged toward the door. "Come on," he said.

Brendan finished gathering the contents of the safe and followed Ducie outside. Sean was kneeling over J.J., who bled from gunshot wounds to his shoulder, torso, and hip.

"How bad is he?" asked Ducie.

"He ain't good," said Sean.

Ducie turned to Brendan. "Give him a hand," he said.

Brendan helped Sean get J.J. to his feet. They followed Ducie toward the back entrance the woman had come from. One by one, they went through an open door leading toward a back alley, passing the woman as she bled out on the pavement. Ducie went to fire a shot into her head, but his gun came up empty; he continued on, ejecting the spent clip from the pistol and shoving a full one in its place.

Brendan's eyes met with the woman's as he passed her. She lay there gasping like a fish out of water, and she looked up at him as if she didn't understand what was happening. Even if an ambulance were to show up at that moment, Brendan knew she didn't have a chance.

He averted his eyes and continued on.

They cut down an alley and hurried toward the lane where Whale waited in the other minivan. Ducie stumbled on his injured leg, and he nearly fell.

"You okay?" asked Brendan.

"Just get to the car," he said.

Sean stopped to help Ducie as Brendan hurried up the alley with J.J. Brendan turned onto a lane and saw a minivan parked in the distance; Whale spotted him when he waved and started opening the minivan's doors. He looked back toward the alley as Brendan approached with J.J.

"Where are the others?" he asked.

"They're coming," said Brendan.

"What the fuck happened?"

Before Brendan could reply, he heard someone shouting in Mandarin. Two uniformed police officers entered the lane from the street with their pistols drawn.

"Look out!" said J.J.

One of the officers fired at them, and something hot and sharp tore through Brendan's left shoulder. It felt as if something had bitten him. At first he wasn't sure what it was—then a bloodstain blossomed on his shirt.

J.J. drew his pistol and returned fire. One of the police officers ducked behind a parked car, and J.J. fired again, exploding a window above him and sending glass showering down. The other officer returned fire and hit Whale in the head, blowing off the top half of his skull. Whale's eyes rolled back to the whites as he slumped to the ground.

"Motherfucker—" Before J.J. could finish, Sean and Ducie emerged from the alley and began firing at the police officers. Ducie hit one of them in the arm, and the man dropped his pistol and shrieked in pain. The other officer returned fire and drove Sean and Ducie back into the alley, pinning them down.

Brendan helped J.J. to his feet as Sean and Ducie exchanged more fire with the officer. They hurried off up one of the narrow back lanes.

CHAPTER FOURTEEN

J.J. leaned on Brendan for support as they rushed up the alley. The front and back of his shirt were slick with blood, and he left an erratic trail of spatter on the wet pavement behind them. Brendan pushed his mask up over his head as he glanced over his shoulder. He turned to J.J.

"You all right?" he asked.

"I'm fucking shot," said J.J.

Brendan pulled J.J. onward.

"This is not good," said J.J. "This is not fucking good at all."

"Just keep moving."

Brendan noticed an elderly woman watching them from a third-story window.

"Where are the others?" asked J.J.

"I don't know."

J.J. stumbled, his shoes sloshing with blood. Brendan strained to hold him up; the pain from his own wound stabbed at his shoulder.

"What the fuck happened back there?" asked J.J.

Before Brendan could reply, a gunshot exploded in the distance. He flinched. After a short silence, three more shots went off in rapid succession, like fireworks.

"Jesus Christ," said J.J. "You think they got tagged?"

Another explosion went off. Brendan wasn't sure whether it was another gunshot or more fireworks. Things fell silent again. He spotted a partially renovated lane house in the distance, inside an open courtyard. Weathered black tarps covered the front door and parts of the upper floors—judging by the amount of dirt that covered the tarps and the building materials in the courtyard, it looked like it had been a while since any work had been done there.

Brendan redoubled his grip on J.J.'s blood-slicked hand and pulled him up higher onto his shoulder, practically hoisting him into a fireman's carry.

"Come on," he said.

They trudged onward toward the lane house. Brendan glanced over his shoulder one more time as they crossed the courtyard to see if anyone was following them, but no one appeared to be. J.J. stumbled on some tiles lying on the trash-strewn floor and nearly fell as they went inside the lane house; Brendan strained to hold him up.

"Careful," he said.

He helped J.J. over toward some bags of concrete in a corner of the room. J.J. collapsed onto the bags as soon as they got there and rolled over onto his back, groaning in pain as he looked up at the ceiling. Brendan took off the mask and tossed it aside.

"Fuck, that hurts," said J.J.

"Let me take a look," said Brendan.

He lifted up J.J.'s blood-soaked shirt, having to peel it back because it was so wet. The entrance wounds on J.J.'s shoulder and hip were small—not much bigger than the size of dimes—and they were through-and-throughs with similar-sized exit wounds, which was a good sign. Even though there was a lot of blood, there was probably a minimal amount of hemorrhaging. The entrance wound of the shot that hit J.J.'s torso was much larger, though: it looked like a wet, red eye. For a moment, Brendan believed that maybe things weren't as bad as he'd first imagined. But when he turned J.J. onto his side and found no exit wound for the torso shot, he knew he was kidding himself. The bullet had either ricocheted or mushroomed inside J.J. and had probably caused major internal damage.

"Goddamn," said J.J., gritting his teeth.

"It's not that bad," said Brendan.

"Are you kidding me? I'm fucking gut-shot."

Brendan lowered J.J.'s shirt back down. He pulled off his own sweatshirt, revealing the gunshot wound on his left shoulder. Compared to J.J.'s injuries, it looked like a scratch. He took out the balisong and fanned it open. Then he began cutting his sweatshirt into pieces.

"Look at all this fucking blood," said J.J.

"I've seen worse."

"Where, in a horror movie?"

"I saw someone get shanked at Rikers. The guy's intestines were spilling out of his side, but they put him back together. He even ended up getting stabbed again the next year, and he survived that, too."

"So they had doctors in there. We don't have shit out here."

"I'll take care of it."

"How?"

"Just let me worry about that."

Brendan began packing squares of his sweatshirt into J.J.'s wounds. J.J. cringed from the pain.

"Goddamn, that hurts," he said. "I knew this was gonna be bad. Fucking knew it. Even read it in my horoscope before we left. 'Don't be afraid to say no to an opportunity,' it said. 'Saying no could mean saying yes to something better.'"

Brendan said nothing.

"Fucking China," said J.J. "We got no business being here."

"Just take it easy."

Brendan finished packing the wounds with pieces of the sweatshirt.

"I'm gonna die here," said J.J.

"You're not gonna die."

Brendan stood up and pulled out his cell phone. He started for the door.

"Where you going?" asked J.J.

"I'm just gonna make a phone call."

"Don't leave me."

"I'm not gonna leave you. I'm just gonna see if I can get some help."

Brendan pulled off his latex gloves and punched in a number on his cell phone as he stepped outside. After a few rings, he got a voicemail message in Mandarin. He hung up and dialed another number; after another moment, a man answered, speaking English with a Swedish accent.

"Jonas?" said Brendan. "It's John. Listen, you don't

know any local doctors, do you? Someone who could make a house call. You know anyone who might? No, that's all right. Thanks anyway."

Brendan hung up and dialed another number. He looked up and then down the alley. It was empty in both directions. Then he looked to the pavement and saw the trail of blood spatter. Even with the rain, it still stood out. He tried to splash some water over it with his foot, but it wouldn't go away.

After a moment, Brendan got another voicemail message. He hung up and called another number, and he got another recording.

"Hamilton? It's—"

He paused, catching himself.

"…John. Listen, I need your help. Give me a call when you get this, okay?"

J.J. shouted from inside the lane house. "Brendan!"

He hung up the cell phone and went back inside. He couldn't believe what he saw. There was so much blood; it looked like the killing floor of a slaughterhouse. He looked to J.J.'s face. All the life had poured out of him, as if he'd aged ten years while Brendan was gone.

"I don't think I'm gonna last much longer," he said.

"Don't say that."

"It's true. I'm fucking dying here. Christ, it hurts. It's not like they say it is at all. It don't feel warm or cold or nothing. It just fucking kills."

"Just try and relax," said Brendan.

He glanced around the room. "You want some water or something?" he asked.

J.J. closed his eyes and gritted his teeth.

"Hang on," said Brendan.

Brendan ran into a bathroom and turned on a faucet. Nothing came out. He went and found a kitchen next and tried the faucet there. After the pipe rattled and the faucet belched up some air, a thin trickle of brown water came forth; a moment later, the water ran clear.

Brendan found an empty plastic bottle among the trash on the floor and rinsed it out. He filled it from the tap and brought it back to J.J., and J.J. drank some of the water, choking on it.

"Go slow."

"You're a good guy, Brendan."

"Just drink."

"No, I mean it. You are."

Brendan said nothing.

"I never thought you ratted," said J.J. "I know how it looked and all, but I never believed it. It just didn't seem like you."

Brendan put down the bottle of water and began cutting more strips from his sweatshirt.

"You remember the time we got in a fight with those guidos down in Bensonhurst?" said J.J. "And they started beating on me with chains and shit? There must have been a dozen of them. Sean and Tommy split, they were so scared—but you didn't. You ran across the street and got that big umbrella and then came running back into the fray and just started swinging. You went berserk, like you were playing Whack-a-Mole."

Brendan said nothing.

"You saved my life that night," said J.J.

"No, I didn't."

"Yeah, you did."

Brendan began changing the soaked bandages with fresh ones. After a moment, J.J. spoke again.

"Listen," he said. "I gotta tell you something."

"What?"

"I don't think that bitch was the one that shot me."

"Just take it easy—"

J.J. reached out and grabbed Brendan by the arm, startling him. "I'm serious, Brendan."

Brendan turned to J.J. He looked sixty years old, slicked with sweat and as gray as an overcooked steak.

"I mean, I know she shot me at least once, but I don't think she was the only one that shot me," said J.J.

"Who else could've shot you?"

"I don't know. It all happened so fast. But the one that hit me in the stomach felt different, and it felt like it came from a different direction. Like from where you guys were standing."

"It couldn't have."

"It did."

"Look, what's done is done," said Brendan. "Now I'm gonna go get us a ride so I can get you out of here and get you fixed up. I'll take you to a vet if I have to, okay? I just need you to keep it together for a few more minutes. Can you do that?"

J.J. nodded, gritting his teeth again. "Promise you won't leave me," he said.

"I'm not gonna leave you," said Brendan. "I'll be right back."

Brendan got up and left the lane house. He made his way toward the nearest side street and looked for a car to steal, spotting a silver Audi sedan. Too new, he thought to himself—it probably had an alarm. Then he spotted an older black Volkswagen Santana parked in another alley across the way.

Brendan pulled out the slim jim as he approached the Santana. He glanced around and made sure no one was watching him. Then he bumped the car—no alarm. He slipped the slim jim between the driver's side window and its rubber seal, and after quickly popping the lock mechanism, he opened the door. Less than thirty seconds later, he had the engine running and pulled away from the curb.

He drove back toward the lane house and parked in the alley behind it. Then he got out of the Santana and left the engine running. He hurried inside, but as he approached J.J., even before he was halfway across the room, he could already tell that he was too late: J.J. was dead.

He lay back on the bags of concrete with his mouth open and his eyes wide, staring blankly at the unfinished ceiling.

Brendan took the pistol from J.J.'s waistband. It had so much blood on it that it nearly slipped out of his hands. After wiping it off on J.J.'s shirt, he checked J.J.'s pockets to see if he had his passport or any other ID on him. He didn't. Brendan slipped the pistol into his own waistband. Then he went back out to the Santana and drove off.

The first thing he had to do was get rid of the diamonds; that much was clear. They were too dangerous to be carrying, and he only made himself a target by having them. He had to find a place to stash them until he figured out what was going on and what his next move should be.

He drove over toward Huashan and then out past Panyu Lu and toward Dingxi, where he knew there were more unfinished construction projects. Luckily for him, Shanghai was always full of them. He found a boarded-up site there at the end of an alley. The plywood that had been used to cover the door and windows was warped and spray-painted over with graffiti; rusted pieces of rebar jutted out like wilted corn stalks from the building's top floors.

He parked across the street from the site and waited for ten minutes, watching to see how often people came and went from the building. During the time he sat there, no one did. He got out of the car and jogged across the street, then pulled back one of the pieces of plywood covering a doorframe and entered the building.

He approached a darkened stairwell. Inside the building, it reeked of urine, turpentine, and mold. He climbed the stairs until he reached the landing on the third floor; there was another floor above him, but it wasn't completed, and the roof was partially open.

He stepped out into a large area and approached an unfinished section of wall. When he looked inside the open wall, he saw an eight-inch gap meant for insulation. He placed the sack of diamonds inside it and covered them with a chunk of drywall.

Brendan left the building and got back into the Santana. He drove back in the direction of his apartment building, going out of his way to avoid anything even remotely near the diamond merchant. The traffic on the streets was worse than normal; it crawled slowly along the wet streets and one-ways.

He scanned the car radio for news as he made his way home. A local station mentioned a robbery in the area, but there weren't many details. Or if there were, they weren't being shared with the public.

A police car swerved around him and screamed past as he headed east on Huaihai Lu, its blue lights flashing and siren wailing as the vehicles in front of him got out of its way. A moment later, another police car barreled by, followed by two police motorcycles. Brendan began to wonder what had happened to Ducie and Sean. Had they gotten away? If so, where were they, and what were they doing? Were they on their way to his place? Were they already there? Another sick feeling grew in the pit of his stomach. Maybe he should call Li, he thought. But what would he say? If they were already there, there was nothing he could do to change that now. But if they weren't there, he was still hoping he wouldn't have to tell her what he'd done, or who he'd been and what he did in the past. He was still hoping to move forward with his life intact and his secrets hidden. He also began to worry about what J.J. had said. Then he wondered if Ducie and Whale had been killed or caught. And if they had gotten caught, would they mention him? Was there anything on either of them that could be linked to him? He began to think about the security guard and the man in the purple suit as well. What had they seen? What were they telling the authorities? There shouldn't have been anything that linked them back at the store; they had been wearing masks and gloves. The guns couldn't be traced to them, and the vehicles weren't theirs, either. But had they made any mistakes? Had they left anything behind? Were there any other cameras that might have picked something up? He went over and over the events in his head.

Then he thought about the woman they'd shot. Surely she must have died. She'd been wounded even worse than J.J. had been, and he was dead. Brendan wondered about the cop that Ducie had shot, too. Had he and Sean had shot any others on their ways out? The authorities must have been scouring the area.

Brendan approached his apartment building. The pain in his shoulder worsened as the adrenalin finally began to dissipate. It felt as if someone was jabbing a sharp instrument into the wound—a steak knife, maybe, or a screwdriver. He slowed the Santana and drove around the block, looking for police, police cars, people in vans, or anything else out of the ordinary. But he noticed nothing strange, so he parked the Santana in an alley on the next block.

Before he got out, he thought about what he would tell Li. She would be surprised to see him; that much was certain. He could tell her the truth, but that would be crazy. If he did, she'd never go with him. She'd probably never forgive him, either. She might even turn him in. Telling the truth was clearly out—he had to make something up. Maybe he could tell her he wanted to surprise her with a vacation, and that he had bought them tickets on the spur of the moment. But he'd never surprised her with anything like that before; it would seem odd and out of character. It might even make her more suspicious. And what if she didn't want to go, or wanted to put it off? It needed to be something more urgent: something necessary that she couldn't say no to. Then it hit him: he would tell her that a family member was dying. An uncle or a cousin who was like a father to him. He would ask her to go along; they might as well bring Xiaodan, too, in case there were other family members present. Li had always wanted to meet his family and friends anyway, and now would be the perfect opportunity. That's what he'd do. He'd tell her that his uncle or cousin lived in Australia, or maybe New Zealand. He'd buy their tickets on the way, and after they got there, he'd figure something else out, some lie or other way to tell her. Maybe he'd even tell her the truth for once, as crazy as that seemed. But whatever he'd end up doing, by then, they would be out of the country, and out of danger.

He got out of the Santana. Then he slowly walked up the

lane toward his apartment building. He saw a light inside their kitchen as he approached the building. He glanced at his watch—it was just before one o'clock, and Li was probably making Xiaodan's lunch, or getting some *fat choy* ready to bring to Yuen's for the reunion dinner.

Brendan entered the building. He unlocked the door to their apartment and went inside.

"Li?"

There was no response. He went into the kitchen, but it was empty. Growing nauseated, he turned around and went back into the other room.

"Hey, babe?" he said. "You home?"

Again, there was no response. He staggered back toward the bedrooms. Maybe they were just out shopping, he thought, or already at Yuen's. His heart began to thud in his chest.

He went into their bedroom: it was empty, too. Then he went into Xiaodan's bedroom. Ducie was sitting there in a rocking chair, with his shin bandaged and a pistol in his hand.

"About fucking time," he said.

CHAPTER FIFTEEN

BRENDAN glanced into the next room. It was empty. He looked back at Ducie.

"Where are they?" he asked.

"Nice to see you, too. Don't I even get a 'hello' or something?"

Brendan drew his pistol and pointed it at Ducie's head. "Where the fuck are they?" he asked.

Ducie raised his own pistol and leveled it at Brendan. "Easy there, cowboy," he said.

"I swear to God—"

Ducie interrupted him. "You swear to God what?" he asked. "You shoot me, and they don't see sundown. Now lower the gun."

Brendan hesitated. Ducie cocked the hammer of the NP-22 and pointed it at Brendan's head.

"Lower the fucking gun or I'll lower it for you," he said.

Brendan hesitated for another moment before finally lowering the pistol.

"That's better," said Ducie, lowering his own pistol.

"What did you do with them?" asked Brendan.

"Nothing yet. But if I don't get my diamonds, that'll change."

"I don't have them."

"What do you mean, you don't have them?"

"I stashed them."

"Why?"

"What do you mean, why? That place was crawling with cops."

"So where are they now?"

"Somewhere safe."

"And J.J.?"

"He's dead."

"You sure?"

"Yeah, I'm sure."

Ducie struggled to stand. "Let's get the stones," he said, starting for the door.

"I'm not going anywhere until I see my family," said Brendan.

Ducie stopped and looked back to Brendan. "You're not the one in charge here," he said.

"Neither are you," said Brendan. "You want to see the diamonds, then let me see my family. Otherwise, you can just shoot me now and get it over with."

Ducie hesitated for a moment, mulling it over as if he was actually considering it.

They left the apartment and made their way up one of the back lanes. Outside, a light rain had resumed falling, and somewhere in the distance, a battery of rockets went off.

Ducie led the way, walking with a limp and trying not to put any weight onto his injured leg. Brendan followed, occasionally glancing over his shoulder to see if anyone was watching or following them. Thoughts raced through his mind, and he had trouble concentrating; he felt as if he'd taken too much speed and had been up all night. He needed to focus, but the more he tried to stop his mind from racing, the more out of control his thoughts became.

They turned onto another back alley and made their way to a narrow and high-walled lane. A few crates of empty beer bottles sat outside the entrance to a kitchen. They passed a small shack where two people sat on folding beach chairs and watched Chinese New Year programming on a television set plugged into a snaking extension cord. Then they passed another shack where a young mother held a baby defecating through slit pants onto a dirty paper plate. No one paid them any attention.

They turned onto another alley when they reached the end of the lane. Brendan's wounded arm was starting to go numb, and it felt like a twenty-five pound dumbbell hanging from his side. Ducie stopped at a rusty metal gate halfway up the alley and pushed it open; it creaked as if it hadn't been moved in years.

Brendan followed Ducie through the gate and into a courtyard full of rusted bicycles, grimy window frames, and other trash. They approached a low door leading into the basement of a run-down lane house. Ducie pushed open the door and went inside, and Brendan followed.

They made their way through a garbage-cluttered basement and approached a narrow stairwell. Then they went upstairs into a cramped room lit by a single battery-powered light bulb. The place smelled like rancid cooking oil, and there didn't appear to be any plumbing or electricity. Mold and grime covered the walls in Rorschach patterns: one looked like a crude map of Russia, and another looked like a horse's head.

Brendan started to wonder where the occupants of the house were and felt nauseated again. He followed Ducie into another small room. Sean was there, sitting on a chair; he had a QSZ-92 pistol in his hand. Li sat on the edge of a fraying couch nearby. She jumped up and rushed toward Brendan as he entered the room.

"*Shénme ta me de?*" she asked, embracing him.

"Don't be talking no chink in here," said Ducie, separating them.

"You all right?" asked Brendan.

Li nodded.

"Where's Xiaodan?" he asked.

Li pointed to the next room. Brendan looked inside. Xiaodan slept underneath a jacket on the lower berth of a bunk bed.

"Who are these people?" asked Li.

Ducie spoke before Brendan could reply. "I want my fucking diamonds," he said.

"What's going on?" asked Li.

"I can explain," said Brendan.

"Save it," said Ducie.

"Let them go."

"No fucking way."

"You want the diamonds, let them go."

"What guarantee do we have you'll give us the stones if we let them go?"

"What guarantee do I have you'll let them go if I do?"

Ducie hesitated.

"Well?" asked Brendan.

"It looks like we've got a Mexican standoff here," said Ducie. "Only I can live without the diamonds. Can you live without them?"

Li turned to Brendan. "What's he talking about, John?" she asked.

"Ain't that cute," said Sean. "She thinks his name's John. I bet she doesn't even know he has a record. Do you, sweetie?"

Brendan spoke before Li could reply. His racing mind finally slowed down, and a plan emerged from all the noise.

"I'll take one of you to the diamonds," he said. "But as soon as we get them, the other one lets my family go."

"Fuck that," said Ducie.

"It's the only way I'm doing this."

"Doing what?" said Li.

Sean spoke before Brendan could reply. "I'll go," he said.

"What?"

"You stay here with her," said Sean. "I'll take him."

"You sure?" asked Ducie.

Sean nodded. "He so much as thinks about stepping out of line, I'll put a bullet in him," he said.

"Get his gun," said Ducie.

Sean took the pistol from Brendan and gave it to Ducie. Li began to speak.

"John—"

Ducie interrupted her. "You've got one hour," he said. "I don't hear back from Sean by then, I'm gonna go Nanking on your little family here. Are we understood?"

Sean shoved Brendan toward the door before he could reply. They made their way down into the basement. Brendan noticed coagulating blood by the bottom of a closet door before they reached the exit, and he realized where the occupants of the house were.

CHAPTER SIXTEEN

S EAN jabbed the pistol into Brendan's back. Waves of dull pain radiated out from the bullet wound in Brendan's shoulder.

"Keep moving," said Sean.

Brendan gritted his teeth and trudged on. They continued along the alley running from Panyu Lu to Fahuazhen, past a row of crumbling lane houses. Overhead, the sky was the color of setting concrete; the streets were still slick with rain, and a noxious-smelling slurry ran in a gutter along the curb.

They turned onto another alley. Brendan's eyes met the tired gaze of an old man sitting inside a small house with a corrugated-steel roof. Could the old man tell he was in trouble? Brendan wondered. And if so, did he care? Wasn't Brendan just another *laowai* in a situation of his own making, repeating the same mistakes of the generations of *laowai* that had come before him?

Before Brendan could get anything across to the old man, Sean shoved him onward. And even if he had been able to get anything across, what would have been the point? There was nothing that the old man could have done. If anything, getting a local involved would have only created more loose ends.

They left the alley and approached a park where a

lone septuagenarian practiced *tai chi*. Brendan could feel the sticky blood seeping like tree sap down his arm. The construction site where he'd stashed the diamonds was only another block away. He thought about stalling, but what good would that do? he wondered. If Sean didn't call Ducie in the next fifteen minutes, Ducie was going to kill Li and Xiaodan.

He continued to check down his list. He could try to fight Sean, but he hadn't fought anyone in years. Would he remember how? And even if he did, would it matter? His right arm was nearly useless, and on top of that, Sean had a gun.

He stopped as they approached the construction site where he'd stashed the diamonds. Then he turned to Sean and nodded toward the building.

"They're in there," he said.

"So what?"

"So call Ducie."

"Not until we get them."

"But I brought you to the building—"

Sean interrupted him. "That wasn't the deal," he said.

"You know he's not gonna let them go."

"You should have thought of that before you got them involved," said Sean, shoving him forward. "Now move."

They entered the building and made their way to the stairwell. Just before reaching it, a stray dog shot out from the darkness. Sean instinctively fired at it, and the bullet punctured the dog's chest, cutting its growl short and killing it instantly.

Sean shoved Brendan toward the stairwell. "Go on," he said.

Brendan went forward and looked down at the dog as he walked past. The entrance wound on the dog's chest looked just like an eye—and just like the entrance wound on J.J.'s torso had looked. There didn't appear to be any exit wound, either.

"Son of a bitch," said Brendan, realizing. "It was you, wasn't it? You shot J.J."

"Get out of here."

"He got hit by a hollow point."

"So what?"

"So that woman wasn't shooting hollow points, but you are."

"What are you, on CSI now?"

"You were the one who ratted on Ducie, too, weren't you?"

Sean smashed Brendan in the back of the head with the butt of the pistol, and Brendan dropped to a knee.

"I hear another word out of you and I'm gonna shoot your ass," he said. "Now move."

They continued on, making their way up to the third floor. Their footsteps echoed throughout the empty structure. Brendan's mind raced again as he scanned the surroundings for a possible weapon; the site was littered with trash and building materials, but there was nothing there that could be of any use.

They made their way up the last few stairs. Brendan thought about all the people he'd seen on television and in movies walking toward the gallows, or to electric chairs, or to gas chambers. He'd always wondered why they never fought more and now realized that maybe they'd been just like him. Maybe they'd also been checking down their options, looking for some possible way out or reprieve up until and even during the moment the noose was being slipped around their necks. Hope was a powerful force—or was it denial? he wondered. And when it all came down to it, weren't they more or less the same thing? Weren't they both the decision to wait rather than the decision to act?

They stepped out onto the third floor landing, to the unfinished section of wall where he'd hidden the diamonds. He glanced around at the surroundings: still nothing he could use to fight, no open sections of floor or exposed pipes or other items he could use to his advantage. Then Brendan thought about the stairwell itself: it was at least fifteen feet down to the next landing, and the landing itself was solid concrete. There was no guarantee they would even survive the fall, but it seemed like a good play. It seemed like the only play he had.

Brendan uttered a quick prayer under his breath as he reached the top step. *Help me. Fuck it. Here goes nothing.* Then instead of stepping forward onto the landing, he spun around toward Sean. What followed happened fast, but it all slowed down for Brendan the way things do for athletes in the zone. Sean raised the pistol. Brendan pushed off the top stair and went airborne. Sean's index finger moved above the trigger. Blood pumped in the brachial artery of Brendan's wounded upper arm as he lifted it. The trigger of the gun moved a few millimeters as Sean squeezed it. Brendan tackled Sean at the waist as the muzzle flashed and the gun went off. The gunshot exploded throughout the building and throughout his ears. And as they went into the air, his heart leapt up into his throat.

Over the years, he had forgotten what that feeling had felt like. The feeling of control in the face of danger, and of having everything he had riding on a situation. The way his heart pounded in his chest, the way the muscles of his throat tightened and restricted his airflow, the way everything intensified and came into sharp focus. He had forgotten all of those things, and he had forgotten something else: how easy it was to take that first step, to make that decision, to take back control.

They flew backward through the air, weightless and suspended above the floor for the briefest of moments before they came crashing down against the stairs. Sean's arm slammed against one of them and the pistol got knocked loose, clattering down toward the landing. Brendan hit another group of stairs with his side and felt one of his ribs break. They tumbled and slid their way down the remainder of the stairs, straining for purchase and swinging blindly at each other, and they crashed to the landing in a heap.

Brendan rolled over onto Sean at the bottom of the stairs and began pummeling him. He tore into Sean with a flurry of short hooks and jabs. Sean covered up and protected his face, and Brendan dug into Sean's sides, ripping uppercut after uppercut into Sean's ribs.

Sean pinched down his arms to protect his torso, and

Brendan grabbed him by the hair. He pulled Sean's head up off the ground and then smashed him in the face with a solid right; Sean's skull bounced against the concrete with a loud crack. Brendan grabbed Sean by the hair again and went to hit him once more, but before he could, Sean bucked him off as if a horse bucking off a rider.

Brendan landed hard on his injured side. Sean rolled over and ended up on top of him before Brendan could react. He lit into Brendan with a flurry of his own: he punched Brendan in the face, breaking Brendan's nose and splitting his lip; he tore into Brendan's ribs, cracking another one with a punishing blow.

Brendan held his hands up to his face and pinched together his elbows and tried to weather the barrage, but it was no use. Sean smashed Brendan in the face with another right cross, and Brendan saw stars. After his vision slowly returned, Brendan glanced over and spotted the pistol on the landing. He swatted for it. It was just out of reach, but he noticed an open section of floor that he had missed on his way up.

Brendan raised his knee up as hard as he could, connecting with Sean's groin. Sean rolled off to his side sucking for air, and Brendan scrambled out from underneath him. Sean got up and lunged, but like a matador, Brendan sidestepped him with a clumsy semi-verónica and shoved him toward the open section of floor. Sean tried to stop in time, but he couldn't, and he plunged through the hole and disappeared into the darkness. A moment later, a loud crash reverberated in the basement three levels below, then nothing but silence.

Brendan took a knee and sucked for air. As soon as he got his breath, he went over and picked up the pistol, then went back up the stairs toward the third floor. He walked over to the unfinished section of wall and found the small black sack. He opened it. Diamonds glittered in the dark folds of the bag like a tiny galaxy of stars.

Brendan shoved the sack of diamonds into his pocket and started down the stairs. After he passed the second floor landing, a cell phone started ringing.

Sean's cell phone had lit up on the floor.

CHAPTER SEVENTEEN

BRENDAN approached the phone. He picked it up but let it ring until it went over to voicemail. He slid the cell phone into his pocket, then checked the chamber of Sean's QSZ-92. Empty. He checked the magazine—three hollow point rounds were left inside. He slid the magazine back into place and loaded a round into the chamber, then flipped on the safety and shoved the pistol into his waistband.

He left the building. Outside, it was raining again. He put on his sunglasses, even though it beginning to get dark, and headed up the alley and turned onto another back lane. Laundry was drying under a plastic shed.

Nobody around, he picked loose a faded black Members Only jacket. He tried it on—a little damp, and maybe a size too small, but better than his bloodstained t-shirt.

He made his way up the alley, toward Fahuazhen, toward the bakery, sticking to lanes and alleys. Each step delivered another punch to his ribs. He stopped twice, wincing, bearing the pain.

On Panyu Lu, he bought a dark blue baseball and pulled it low over his eyes. He continued on.

It was just before five o'clock when he got to the bakery. They'd closed early for the day, since it was New Year's Eve.

Jessie had already gone home, and Hamilton was cleaning up in the kitchen; Cantopop music was playing on the stereo. Brendan startled him as he entered.

"I wasn't expecting you, sir," said Hamilton, shutting off the music. "I was just about to put everything away."

"That's all right," said Brendan. "I'll get it."

"You sure?"

Brendan nodded as he walked past Hamilton and approached the sink. "You can go now," he said.

"Sir—?"

"It's okay," said Brendan. "I'll finish this."

He kept his back to Hamilton as he scrubbed his hands; the pain was excruciating.

"Did something happen to you?" asked Hamilton.

"I just fell," he said. "That's all."

"Are you sure?"

"I'm fine."

Blood seeping down Brendan's arm mixed with the running water, turning it a faint pink. Brendan increased the water flow to wash it away.

"Go on," said Brendan. "I'll see you on Monday."

"All right," said Hamilton. "Happy new year, sir."

"You, too."

Brendan dried off and entered the pantry. He waited until he heard the back door close behind Hamilton, then slumped to the floor.

Brendan sat there for a few minutes with his eyes closed. Every inch of his body felt as if it was on fire. He would have given anything for some painkillers, or even just a fifth of Jameson's. Then he remembered Li and Xiaodan, and he remembered Ducie. He opened his eyes and struggled to his feet.

He got a roll of plastic wrap from the kitchen and went into the bathroom and turned on the light. He took off the jacket and hung it up on a hook on the back of the bathroom door. After he removed the sunglasses and cap, he carefully peeled off the blood-soaked t-shirt and set it aside on the sink. Then he looked up at his reflection in the mirror, hardly recognizing the face that stared back at him: his broken nose was swollen to twice its normal size and looked as if it had been pushed an inch to the right; both eyes were blackened; and a large, kidney-shaped welt marred the left side of his face. Blackish blood oozed out from a nickel-sized hole on his left shoulder, and his torso was tattooed with bruises.

He turned on the faucet and washed out as much of the blood from his t-shirt as he could until the water finally ran clear. Then he wrung out the t-shirt and set it aside. He folded up some paper towels and pressed them to the bullet wound, then wrapped plastic wrap around his shoulder and arm until the makeshift bandage was secure.

Sean's cell phone rang again as Brendan pulled the t-shirt back on. He took it out and looked at it. He took a deep breath and then slowly let it out, then raised the cell phone to his ear.

After a moment, Ducie answered. "Well," he said. "Did you get rid of him?"

"Yeah," said Brendan. "I did."

Ducie hesitated. "You motherfucker—"

"You should be thanking me," he said. "He's the one who ratted you out, and he killed J.J., too."

"I swear to God—"

"Shut up," said Brendan. "You're not in charge anymore. I am, so listen up. First, you're gonna let my daughter go."

"What?"

"You're not gonna see me or the diamonds until she's safe."

"Go fuck yourself."

"I'm not asking you, I'm telling you. If she's not out on the street in five minutes, I'm going to the police."

"I'll fucking kill both of them right now."

"Go ahead. You'll end up with nothing. You weren't planning on letting us live anyway, so I don't give a fuck what you do."

"You motherfucker—"

"You've got five minutes," Brendan said. "If I don't see my daughter out by the intersection of Hunan and Xingguo by then, you'll never see me or the diamonds again."

Brendan hung up without waiting for a reply. Then he turned off the cell phone.

"Bravo."

He looked up into the mirror. Tommy was standing next to him in the reflection, blood seeping through the holes in his Cookie Monster mask.

"You're getting pretty good at this," said Tommy. "Just like your old self again."

Brendan said nothing.

"You even sounded a bit like Clint Eastwood there," Tommy said. "'I'm not asking you, I'm telling you.' Too bad the jig's up, though. Even if you do pull this off, she still knows you're not John."

"Shut up," said Brendan.

"I wouldn't worry about it," said Tommy. "The chances of you pulling this off are pretty slim, anyway—"

"I said shut up!"

Brendan spun around to face Tommy, but there was no one there.

He went into the kitchen and hid the diamonds in the microwave. Then he started for the door, but he stopped at the Blodgett Zephaire. He went over to the oven and reached behind it, feeling around for the hose connected to the gas line.

As soon as he found it, he yanked it free.

CHAPTER EIGHTEEN

E waited in an alley where he couldn't be seen from the street and watched the intersection of Hunan and Xingguo. A minute went by, then two, then five. Overhead, the sky darkened to the color of a bruise.

He pulled a rumpled cigarette from his battered pack and raised it to his lips. Then he lit it and took a long drag. By the time he finished the cigarette, Ducie would be fifteen minutes late and would be calling his bluff, which meant he was either gone, or the police were on their way, or Li and Xiaodan were dead. Or maybe it meant all three of those things, or worse.

Brendan took the last drag off his cigarette and stubbed it out beneath the toe of his boot. Before he could cross the street, he spotted a small figure emerging from the shadows of one of the back lanes across the way, tottering forward into a pool of light cast by one of the street lamps. He immediately recognized the figure.

"Xiaodan!" he shouted.

She looked up at him when she heard his voice. Judging by the frightened look in her eyes, it was clear that she either didn't recognize his beaten and swollen face or she was terrified of his appearance. She shook her head and backed away from him as he approached.

"Mama!" she said.

He ran after her and scooped her up into his arms. "It's me," he said. "*Bàba.*"

She shook her head again and again and began to cry. He cradled her to his chest and held her tight as he made his way up the block toward Yuen's apartment; she kicked and screamed the entire way. He rang the buzzer when he finally reached the apartment building and set her down by the front door.

"Wait here for *nai nai*, okay?" he said.

A light went on inside the building. Brendan bent down to kiss Xiaodan on the forehead.

"I love you," he said.

Then he turned and hurried off.

Brendan walked up the alley toward the house where Ducie was holding Li. He moved the pistol from the back of his waistband to the front. Then he shifted it from the right side to the left, looking for the spot he could most easily reach it.

He stopped when he arrived at the rusty metal gate and pushed it open as slowly as he could so he wouldn't make much noise. Then he went into the courtyard. Once there, he noticed a light burning inside.

Brendan went in through the low door. He drew the pistol and made his way through the darkened basement and toward the narrow stairwell, ignoring the coagulating blood around the bottom of the closet door. He went upstairs into the kitchen, but there was no one there. He went into the living room—there was no one there, either.

He grew nervous. Was it a setup?

"Li?" he said.

There was no reply. He continued on, approaching another stairwell that led to the second floor. He held the pistol at his side as he went up the stairs, his index finger hovering just above the trigger. At the top of the stairs, he saw a light burning in what appeared to be a bathroom at the end of a hallway. He called out again.

"Hello?"

There was still no reply. Brendan raised the pistol and approached the bathroom door, then stepped inside the bathroom with the pistol leveled before him. He froze when he saw Li standing underneath a shower faucet on her tiptoes, bound and gagged. One end of a noose was tied to the showerhead, while the other end was tied tightly around her neck.

"Li—"

Her eyes bulged out of their sockets when she saw Brendan. She tried to tell him something, but the gag muffled her words. She gestured toward something behind him, but before he could turn around, Ducie pistol-whipped him in the side of the head.

"You motherfucker," said Ducie.

Brendan dropped to a knee. Ducie pistol-whipped him in the face, breaking one of Brendan's teeth. Brendan dropped his pistol, and Ducie kicked it away. Then he took the balisong from Brendan's pocket.

"Where are the diamonds?" asked Ducie, frisking him.

"I don't have them."

"Bullshit."

"I don't, I swear—"

Ducie pistol-whipped Brendan in the face again. "Motherfucker," he said.

"Please," said Brendan, spitting the words through blood and bits of teeth. "Let her go—"

Ducie grabbed Brendan by the hair and yanked him to his feet. "Get the fuck up," he said

He pushed Brendan out into the hall. Brendan staggered toward the stairwell, cradling his injured ribcage. Ducie shoved him on, limping after him.

Behind them, Li groaned through the gag as she struggled to stay on her toes.

They left the house and walked up the alley. Brendan clutched his side as he led the way. His right eye was swollen shut, and he could barely see out of his left. It hurt to breathe in; each time he inhaled, it felt as if he was being stretched on a rack. His mouth was full of blood and grit, and he was bleeding from too many wounds to count. He couldn't help but think of the black and white *língchí* photographs he'd seen in an old book, where Chinese criminals were slowly dismembered alive in a process known as death by a thousand cuts.

They stayed on the unlit back lanes and alleys. Ducie kept the gun on Brendan, holding it inside a jacket pocket. Brendan rehearsed things in his mind as they approached the front door of the bakery. When he put his hand in his pocket to get his keys, he would also take out his lighter, hiding it in his palm. After they were inside, he would lead Ducie toward the kitchen, where Brendan would strike the lighter—and the place would explode. He hoped there wasn't so much gas that the blast would kill them both, but it was a risk he was willing to take.

They reached the end of the lane, and Brendan nodded to the bakery across the way.

"They're in there," he said.

Ducie shoved Brendan forward. "Go on," he said.

Brendan led Ducie toward the front door of the bakery. He reached into his pocket for the keys.

"You try anything, and I swear to God, I'm gonna go back there and disembowel your wife," said Ducie. "Then I'll go find that daughter of yours and do the same thing to her."

Brendan said nothing as he palmed the lighter and pulled out the keys. His hand trembled as he raised the keys toward the lock. He took a deep breath and let it out slowly, and his hand stopped shaking. Then he slid the key into the lock and opened the door.

They went inside. Ducie followed Brendan, keeping his hand on the pistol in his pocket. They made their way back toward the kitchen. Before long, Brendan could smell the gas. *Just a few more steps*, he thought to himself, *and this will all be over.*

Before they reached the kitchen, Ducie noticed the gas as well. Brendan saw it register in Ducie's eyes, and he went to strike the lighter, but before he could, Ducie grabbed his wrist.

"You son of a bitch," said Ducie.

Ducie seized Brendan by the back of the neck with his other hand and shoved him face-first into the wall. He twisted Brendan's wrist back behind him and wrenched it up into an arm bar. Brendan dropped the lighter, and Ducie kicked it skittering across the floor.

"*Where are my fucking diamonds?*" shouted Ducie.

Brendan mule-kicked his heel up into Ducie's groin and pulled free as Ducie dropped to his knees. He went for the lighter, but before he could get to it, Ducie sprang to his feet and tackled him from behind. They hit the floor in a heap, and Ducie flipped Brendan onto his back and began to pummel him.

Brendan turned and looked for the lighter. Through a swollen eye, he saw it lying on the floor only a few feet away. He swatted for it, but it was just out of reach. Ducie punched him in the face again, and Brendan's head snapped back against the floor and cracked against the tile. He saw bright stars and heard ringing in his ears—everything was blurry and off, like the images of a burned reel of film.

Before he could reach for the lighter again, Ducie grabbed him by the throat and began to squeeze.

"Give me my diamonds," said Ducie, punctuating each word by smashing Brendan's head into the floor. "Now!"

Brendan swatted for the lighter one more time, but it

was still just out of reach. He began to asphyxiate as Ducie continued to choke him. He looked up at Ducie's face, and for a moment, it almost seemed as if he was staring into a mirror somehow—like some exaggerated, carnival funhouse mirror. He suddenly felt sick.

Things started to go black. Then Brendan felt the balisong in Ducie's pocket as Ducie leaned over him. He shot up a hand and fished it out from Ducie's pocket, then fumbled it open and swung it with every last bit of energy he could muster, slamming it home into one of Ducie's kidneys.

Ducie groaned in pain. He released his grip on Brendan's throat and reached for his lower back as if he'd been shot there. Brendan scrambled out from underneath him, gasping for air. With his free hand, Ducie reached into his jacket pocket for the pistol, but Brendan punched him in the face before he could, and the pistol fell clattering to the floor.

Brendan snatched up the pistol before Ducie could get to it. Ducie looked up at him, more surprised than anything else.

"You son of a—"

Before Ducie could finish, Brendan fired a single shot into Ducie's temple. Ducie fell backward to the floor in a heap, and an uneven halo of dark blood began spreading across the tile floor beneath his head.

Brendan wiped the handle of the pistol with his shirt, then knelt down and put the pistol in Ducie's right hand. He made his way back into the kitchen, where he opened the windows and door and shut off the gas. Then he reached inside the microwave and pulled out the bag of diamonds.

He made his way to the exit door and left the bakery, but before he got far, he heard a voice behind him:

"Don't fucking move."

CHAPTER NINETEEN

BRENDAN started to turn around, but before he could see who it was behind him, he got hit in the side of the head with a blunt object.

"What part of 'Don't fucking move' did you not understand?" said Sean.

Brendan fell to his knees. He saw bright spots of light again, and he heard a tinny ringing in his ears. Sean frisked him while he was down and took the diamonds and pistol from him. Brendan shook his head until he could see straight again and then looked up. Sean's face was a mess. His clavicle was badly fractured and his shoulder was separated, and his right arm dropped a few inches lower than his left and hung limply at his side. He pointed the pistol at Brendan with his good hand and leaned on a golf club for support with the other.

"Bet you thought you saw the last of me," he said.

Brendan moved to get up.

"Not so fast," said Sean, cocking the hammer of the pistol. He fished a bloody slim jim from his waistband and tossed it at Brendan's feet.

"Go on," he said. "Get us some wheels."

Brendan broke into another Volkswagen Santana; they were everywhere, and they were easy enough to steal. Sean got into the passenger's seat next to him, keeping the pistol pointed at him the entire time.

Brendan hotwired the car and got the engine started. They drove off and made their way toward one of the elevated rings leading out of the city. There was little traffic on the streets, and it was dark outside. Every minute or two, another battery of fireworks went off in the distance. The colorful explosions lit up the nighttime sky.

"I didn't think you had it in you," said Sean. "I thought I could use you to help me get rid of Ducie, but I didn't think you'd actually do it."

Brendan said nothing.

"You did actually get rid of him, right?"

Before Brendan could reply, Sean spoke again, laughing. "I'm just fucking with you," he said. "I saw you shoot him in the head. Still, you might want to do a better job of checking next time. You'd avoid any awkward situations like this."

Brendan put on his turn signal when they approached an exit for the highway to Ningbo, but Sean reached over and flipped it off.

"Easy there," he said.

"I thought we were going to Ningbo?" asked Brendan.

"You thought wrong," said Sean. "We were never going to Ningbo. Just keep heading north."

"You had this planned from the start, didn't you?"

"It's a dog-eat-dog world, bro," said Sean. "Don't act so surprised."

They drove on in silence. Brendan struggled to come up with a plan. He could try to overpower Sean, but Sean had a gun. He could go along to wherever Sean was taking him, but there was no guarantee Sean would let him walk away. If anything, it seemed unlikely, as Brendan was the only other remaining member of their group. Before he could come up with a plan, a massive red horsetail shell burst and broke in the sky ahead of them. Then a trio of multi-breakers went off to their right, glittering like waterfalls as they fell away.

"We're getting close now," said Sean. "The Year of the Tiger."

Brendan said nothing. He scanned the road ahead of him and checked the rear and side view mirrors.

"You know the story of how the zodiac came to be, don't you?" said Sean.

Brendan shook his head.

"How can you live in China and not know about the great race?" asked Sean.

Again, Brendan did not reply. Sean found a pack of cigarettes in the glove compartment.

"My *nai nai* used to tell me all them stories when I was a kid," he said.

He lit a cigarette and took a deep drag before continuing.

"Back in the day, they were trying to come up with a calendar," he said. "The Jade Emperor called a meeting of the animals. He put it across this river and said the years on the calendar would be named for each animal in the order they arrived. So all the animals set out. The rat and the cat weren't good swimmers, but they managed to talk the ox into giving them a ride across. But halfway across the river, the rat pushed the cat into the water. Then when they got close to shore, he jumped off the ox's back and got to the meeting place first. That's why the rat's the first sign of the zodiac."

Brendan said nothing.

"Sure seems fitting here, doesn't it?" said Sean. "You did all the heavy lifting, and now it looks like I'm gonna win the race."

Again, Brendan said nothing.

"You're not an ox, are you?" asked Sean.

Brendan didn't reply.

"That's okay," said Sean. "You don't have to answer. I'm not a rat. Sure, I ratted on Ducie, but that's different. That motherfucker had it coming. Me, I'm actually a dragon. You know—strong, passionate, decisive. Everything you're not. Us dragons are generous, too. Did you know that? And I'm gonna be true to my nature, even though I don't believe in that hokey peasant bullshit. I'm gonna let that wife and kid of yours live, unlike Ducie, who probably would have slit their throats as soon as he got the diamonds. You should be happy I pulled this off. At least they'll get out of this all right. Hell, I bet they won't even end up missing you that much. Maybe they will at the start, but in a few years? That little girl won't even remember who you were. They never really even knew you anyway, did they? You were just a lie. A fucking *gweilo*."

Sean pointed to an approaching exit. "Turn off there," he said.

Brendan put on his turn signal and slowed down to get off at the exit. Then he spotted a divider by the exit, and he got an idea. Instead of slowing down, he stomped down on the accelerator.

"What are you doing?" asked Sean. "Slow down."

Brendan stepped down even harder on the accelerator, pressing it to the floor.

"Hey," said Sean. "Slow the fuck down…"

Before Sean could finish, Brendan swerved and hit the divider head on. The front of the car crumpled in a cacophony of crunching glass and steel. Brendan's forehead smashed against the steering wheel while Sean went face-first into the dashboard. The horn switch broke and the horn continued to blare long after Brendan lifted his head from the wheel.

"Motherfucker," said Sean, blood gushing from his mouth and nostrils.

Brendan reached over and grabbed Sean's seatbelt and looped it around his neck. Then he pulled it taut. Sean dropped the pistol and reached up for the seatbelt and began clawing at it; his eyes bulged from their sockets. Brendan pulled as tightly on the makeshift garrote as he could. Sean began to slap and flail at him. He kicked at Brendan, then at the dash and the windshield, spider-webbing the glass. Brendan pulled tighter and leaned away with all his weight, and Sean continued to kick and flail and wheeze for a moment, making a sound like a cat coughing up a hairball. Then he made a sound like an inflatable mattress losing its air. Then nothing. Then Sean finally stopped fighting and went slack. Brendan held tight for another full minute, and when he finally let go, he knew without a doubt that Sean was dead.

Brendan took the sack of diamonds and the pistol from Sean and forced open his door.

He got out and limped off down the exit ramp.

CHAPTER TWENTY

BRENDAN stole another car and drove back toward the Huangpu district. Fireworks continued to erupt over the city with more frequency as midnight approached. There were peonies and willows. Kamuros and crossettes. Bengal fire and bouquet shells. The skies over Shanghai were like a giant Lite-Brite board, exploding with color.

Brendan parked the car a block from the house where Li was being held. The streets were empty aside from a few individuals and small groups lighting off more fireworks. He went inside the house but found the bathroom empty and the untied noose at the bottom of the shower stall: Li was nowhere to be seen.

He left the house and walked back to their apartment building on foot, keeping to the unlit back lanes and side streets. The air smelled like sulfur and burnt paper. The rain had finally stopped, and most of the rainwater was swirling along the gutters and down the drains. His entire body hurt, but he was getting numb to the pain, or at least just used to it.

He soon reached their apartment building. He walked around the block to see if there were any police cars waiting for him there, but there weren't. Then he went inside, but he didn't find Li and Xiaodan there, either.

He went into the bedroom and put on a pair of clean jeans and a plain black jacket. He packed a quick bag, throwing a change of clothes into it for Li and Xiaodan as well. As soon as he was finished packing, he went into the closet and moved aside the ceiling panel, then reached into the darkness for his leather toiletry kit. He started to panic when he didn't initially find it, but then he felt his fingertips brush against its scuffed leather hide.

He began to feel optimistic as he made his way to Yuen's apartment. For the first time since Sean and the others had arrived, he could see a light at the end of the tunnel. Perhaps things would work out after all, he thought. Perhaps his time in Shanghai would not end as badly as it had ended in New York City.

He walked around the block when he got to Yuen's apartment building and looked to see if there were any police cars there as well. There weren't. Then he approached the door and pressed the buzzer. After a moment, Yuen's voice came over the intercom's speaker.

"*Wei?*"

He tried to reply in Mandarin. "Where's Li?" he asked.

"*Zou kai.*"

"I need to speak to her."

"*Zou kai!*" shouted Yuen.

He started to respond in Mandarin before switching over to English. "Open this fucking door," he said. "Now."

Yuen responded in English. "She no want to see you," she said. "Now go."

Brendan pounded against the door. "Li!" he shouted. "I'm not leaving until I talk to you."

"I call police!"

"Open up!"

He continued to pound against the door. "Li!"

Brendan heard a voice from above. "Go away!"

He looked up and saw her in a third floor window. She looked like an angel in the dim, hazy light of the sodium-vapor street lamps. There was a bruise on one side of her face, and her eyes were red and puffy from crying.

"Please—"

"You're a liar," she said, interrupting him. "And a thief. And God knows what else."

"I'm sorry—"

"We could have been killed!"

He said nothing.

"I never want to see you again," she said. "If you so much as step within a hundred feet of my daughter, I'll kill you myself. Do you understand me?"

"Wait—"

"Just go away!" she shouted.

She slammed the window closed before he could reply, and he stood there for a long moment, staring at the empty space where she'd just been standing. Before long, he heard police sirens approaching in the distance.

He turned and disappeared into the shadows.

CHAPTER TWENTY-ONE

BRENDAN walked south toward Huangpi Bei Lu, in the direction leading away from Tomorrow City. He felt lightheaded and weak from the loss of blood; he stopped once to throw up and another time just to sit at a bus stop and catch his breath.

He continued heading south toward Guangchang Park. Fireworks erupted in the sky above and all around him, but he was oblivious to them. He found a half-finished construction site near the intersection of Jiangyin and Chongking and went inside. After he found an empty room on the second floor, he took out his cell and started to dial the number of the dealer he'd purchased the fake passport from, but he stopped halfway through, afraid the authorities might be trying to locate him through his phone. He took out the phone's battery and tossed both it and the phone into a dumpster, then pulled out the burner Ducie had given him and dialed the dealer's number. After a few rings, the dealer answered.

"*Wei?*"

"It's John."

"Who?"

"The American," said Brendan, unable to remember if

he'd used his real name in their dealings. "You sold me a passport."

The dealer said nothing.

"I need help getting out of the country," said Brendan.

The dealer told him he'd see what he could do and would call him back. Four hours later, the cell phone rang, waking Brendan, who'd fallen asleep sitting up. A skein of dried blood peeled away from his cheek as he raised his head from where it had been resting against the wall. He couldn't move three of the fingers on his right hand—they'd become as swollen as sausages—so he answered the phone with his left. It was the dealer, returning his call. He told Brendan he'd called a snakehead he knew; for fifty thousand *kuài*, the snakehead could take Brendan out of the country with some Fujianese emigrants he was bringing to America. Brendan agreed to the price, and the dealer sent a car to the construction site.

A few minutes after he got picked up, Brendan passed out in the back seat of the car.

The driver took Brendan to a doctor in Suzhou to treat his wounds. He ended up having two broken ribs, three broken fingers, a concussion, a sprained ankle, and a lacerated spleen. For another fifty thousand *kuài*, the doctor treated Brendan's injuries and gave him a blood transfusion, and Brendan spent the following ten days recovering in the attic of the doctor's house.

Before he left China, Brendan anonymously returned

the diamonds to the merchant, except for a four-carat stone he kept for himself. He put the rest of them in a large padded envelope with no return address on it and dropped it into a China Post mailbox. He also kept eighty thousand *kuài* from the stash he'd been keeping in his leather toiletry bag, but he sent everything else to Li and Xiaodan in another large padded envelope with no return address.

Brendan met the snakehead at a Sinopec station on the outskirts of Suzhou. They traveled south by bus to the city of Kunming, a day's drive from the Burmese border. In Kunming, they stayed in a run-down hotel for five days, packed six people to a room; they watched Chinese soap operas and game shows on a small black and white television set, and they ate nothing but peanuts and watery rice.

Just after midnight on the fifth night, the snakehead woke them and made them hide in the back of a truck behind some sacks of grain. He drove them within a few miles of the Burmese border, and from there, they set off on foot into the wilderness. It took three weeks to cross over the Bago Yoma mountain range. Brendan ended up getting sick during the journey and lost almost twenty pounds, but it could have been worse: one of the older emigrants collapsed and died along the way. In keeping with Fujianese peasant traditions, they buried the man's body near an old tree on the side of a nameless hill.

After he arrived in Burma, Brendan left the snakehead in Lashio and arranged for a ride to Tachilek, a small town near the borders of Thailand and Laos. He rode in the back of rickety Toyota pickup truck full of migrant workers and monks, worrying about what would happen at the border when they discovered his stolen passport had neither exit stamps for China nor entry stamps for Laos. When he arrived in Tachilek, he could see Thailand and Laos across the Mekong River; a group of German backpackers were going through a customs checkpoint at a bridge. Brendan followed the group and handed his passport to a pair of border guards armed with RPK machine guns. The guards let the Germans through, but there was something wrong with Brendan's passport: they shook their heads and pointed at the empty pages in the back of the passport and angrily questioned him in Burmese.

Brendan pleaded to them in English first, and then in Mandarin, but they understood neither language. They called over another pair of guards sharing a cigarette nearby, and they all had a conference. They kept shaking their heads and taking turns looking over the passport. Finally, one of the second group of guards approached Brendan; the man spoke some English.

"Where's your entry visa?" he asked.

"I don't know," said Brendan. "I went through customs at Lashio. No one stamped my passport there."

The man didn't seem to believe him.

"You're missing your permit to leave Burma," he said.

"No one mentioned anything at the MTT office," said Brendan.

The man shook his head and went back to have another conference with the others. Brendan looked for a place to run or to hide, but they were out in the open, and there were more armed border guards at the bridge and outside the MTT office. After a long moment, the guard who spoke some English finally returned from the conference with the others.

"You have to go back to the MTT office in Mandalay—unless you can come up with the money for the visa fees and the additional processing fee," he said.

"How much is that?" asked Brendan.

"How much do you have?"

Brendan took out his wallet and showed the guard his cash. The guard looked it over before returning to the others for another conference. After a long moment, he returned, accepted Brendan's money, and gave him an exit visa.

Brendan took a boat across the river and into Laos. At Xieng Kok, he got a bus to Cambodia, which he knew had some of the least cooperative extradition policies in the world; he paid for his ticket with some emergency money he'd hidden underneath the sole of one of his shoes. When he got to the border of Laos and Cambodia, he went through a similar show with the border guards there, but with the proper stamps from Burma, all he had to do was pay for an entry visa, and they let him into the country.

He made his way to Phnom Penh, and when he got there, he spent the last of his money on a bowl of noodles from a street vendor and a room in a rundown hotel. He slept for fourteen hours—even the constant riot of moto-dups and *tuk-tuks* outside his window could not wake him.

The following afternoon, he sold the diamond to a Camko City jeweler for $40,000. The diamond was easily worth three times that much, but he didn't care: he knew that he could live for a long time in Cambodia on forty grand.

He continued on toward the southern coast, and he stopped when he found a small one-bedroom apartment for rent in a village near Sihanoukville. Construction cranes dotted the landscape; factories and hotels were going up in every direction. Like Shanghai, it was another tomorrow city, a landscape in flux, growing fast enough for there to be opportunities, but not so fast that a person couldn't remain out of sight. He bought a business visa and found a small empty store for rent only a few hundred yards from the beach, within walking distance of some new Western hotels that had already opened. It wasn't as big or as nice as his last bakery was, or even his first bakery in Queens, but it would do.

He bought a used convection oven from a nearby hotel in the process of upgrading its kitchen appliances, and within a month, just as the rainy season came to an end and the tourists started to return, he was open for business again. He catered to Westerners, offering coffee, pastries, and bread. By late summer, he was making a profit, and by November he was able to hire a local to help him run the place. He tried to wire some money into Li's account bank in Shanghai, but a bank employee told him the account had been closed. He gave some money to the snakehead to give to Li or her mother, but after a month, the snakehead told him he couldn't find either one and returned the money.

They were no longer at their old addresses, and their cell phones were no longer in service: they'd disappeared from Shanghai just like he had, without a trace.

As the Year of the Tiger came to a close, Brendan got a new tattoo of a tiger on the inside of his left forearm, in the same spot where his former tattoo had been. He got it in the flowing, colorful style of Cambodia, and he added Li and Xiaodan's names below it in Khmer script. He threw himself into his work; business was good, and by the following summer, he was able to hire another local. He started donating bread to a nearby orphanage and to a clinic for sex workers with AIDS; he knew it wouldn't change his past or erase the things he'd done, but he no longer cared. There was nothing that could be done about that, anyway— the only thing to do was to keep moving forward, as Richie had told him to do.

Every now and then, Brendan would see a child on the beach who would remind him of Xiaodan. Perhaps he'd see a young girl with long black hair, or he'd see someone with eyes that reminded him of hers. For a brief moment, he would imagine that Li and Xiaodan were coming back to be with him, coming to give him another chance and to start over again together, for real and with no secrets between them.

But the child would always run on toward a mother who looked nothing like Li, and Brendan would return again to his kitchen.

ACKNOWLEDGMENTS

F IRST and foremost, thanks to Marshall Moore, Justin Nicholes, Justin Kowalczuk, Shannon Young, and everyone else at Signal 8 Press and Typhoon Media.

Thanks also to Robert Tregenza, Tom Gresham, Toni-Leslie James, and all of my colleagues and students at Virginia Commonwealth University's School of the Arts.

Thanks to Aaron Henry, Chuck Stephenson, Chris Stanton, Doug Miro, Carlo Bernard, Dan Forman, Jon Paquette, Brian Peterson, Kelly Souders, Diego Canedo, Paul Foley, Dave Boerger, Eric Newman, Mark Shepherd, David Weber, Frank Daniel, and everyone else at USC. And thanks to Ross Gay, Lee Upton, Dan Krzyzkowski, Gladstone Hutchinson, Hal Hochman, and everyone else at Lafayette College.

Thanks to Darrell Fusaro, Kevin Giordano, Kohl Sudduth, Rod Sweitzer, Matt Sweesy, James Lavin, Scott Messina, Andrew Wheelwright, Dag Roland, Rob Harriell, Trevor Long, Paul Desantis, Dan Safarik, Thomas Riermeier,

Paul Niehues, Philip Gostelow, Ed and Nancy Turner, and the LaCroix family.

Many thanks to Huang Ya Ming, Hanson Zhu, David Kao, Milton Lu, James Zhang, Chen Fan, and all of the people of Shanghai and China for your hospitality and generosity. I apologize for any inaccuracies or misrepresentations of China in this story—this is a work of fiction, not fact, based on one outsider's limited experience.

And last but not least, and perhaps most of all, thanks to my family: Lauren, Amalie, Anfinn, Kristen, Richard, Kathryn, Eric, the Kjeldsens, the Zacharys, the Schultes, the O'Briens, and the Davidsons. I love you all.

CPSIA information can be obtained at www.ICGtesting.com
Printed in the USA
LVOW07s2232270514

387528LV00014B/197/P